Of Fish and Folk: Book 1

BY JANET SWAN

Self-published using the *CreateSpace* platform

ISBN-13:9-781482-515589

Of Fish and Folk: Book 1

How can we tell where we are going if someone does not tell us the story of where we have come from?

Prologue

D idey, Didey, tell us a story aboot long ago!" we chorused together, my twin brother and I. My maternal grandfather would smile; remove his spectacles, clean them with his hanky from his trouser pocket, replace them on his nose and begin, in the same way he always did, "Well, the auld folkies used tae say…"

It was the 31st of December, the raw, ragged tail of the year and a howling gale whirled around the tiny fishing village on the North East coast of Scotland where our grandparents lived. We were ten years old, James and I, but no Hogmanay television shows or late night feasts for us, oh no! All we wished was to see in the New Year with Didey John and Granny Maggie while our little sister, Mary was already in her bed at home.

We sat before the fire on two little three-legged wooden stools which our great-uncle, Maggie's brother Alexander, had made for us in his old mending loft. The tongues of flame leapt up in the grate, bright yellow, red and orange, tinged with blue, a mesmerising sight for two twentieth-century children brought up with central heating. The fire seemed to be a gateway into the past, a visual symbol for the stories our grandfather told us. Tales of stormy seas, broken masts, torn nets, curious fish and far-away fishing grounds were more magical that any department store Santa's grotto could ever have been.

This particular Hogmanay, after our schoolteacher Mrs Gibson had been reading Dickens' A Christmas Carol to the class over the last weeks of the term, James and I were very keen on ghost stories. But it was James who had the nerve to ask, "Didey, can you tell us a ghost story? A true one?"

"Didey" John Slater looked at us with a little smile, "Ghosts? Aye, yes, I had a queer experience when I was a boy, nae much younger than you, James," Didey began.

Granny Maggie was sitting in the armchair opposite, knitting as ever, her cleaning done early so she could look after us. "Ye weren't at the sea then, John, no," she said.

"No, no, I wis still at school. I was coming hame fae the chip shop, just doon the lane at the heid o this hoose, and I saw the man fa bade in the next hoose sitting on his window sill ootside. It was nae richt dark, so I saw him clear as a bead. He waved as I came down the lane between the hooses, and I waved back and shouted hello. Well, I came in to my mither's kitchen, carrying the chips and said tae her 'I've just seen the mannie next door, sitting on his window sill,' and she just looked at me, 'Oh no, John, ye canna have seen him, that man is in his bed at death's door!' and she meant it. But I said 'No, Mam, I saw him, clear as anything, am nae telling a lie!' 'Well,' she said, 'If ye did, that's afore something!' And the next morning, we were told by the mannie's wife that he'd passed away in the nicht. And that wis my experience!" Didey always did this, told stories concisely with no embellishment.

"Ooh!" I shrieked, "So it was him that you saw? The man was a ghost!"

Didey smiled knowingly.

"Were there any other stories like that, Didey? Were there any ghosts long ago?" James chimed in, following my train of thought perfectly as ever.

"Well, I've heard o' a man that went doon to the shore tae check on his boat, they aa had wee yoles, sailing boats awa back… and it had been a very poor day and nicht, the fishermen could hardly get oot tae sea for the weather… but this man was doon there and he saw another man he knew, leaning across een o the other boats. He rose up to speak tae him, but the man wis nae longer there when he looked. And he thought, 'That's afore something, we'll hear bad news this day', and so, when the boats did come back later in the morning', there was a man lost out of een o them."

"No way! So, the man had died at the time he'd been seen? Aye?" I persisted, thinking of how Dickens' ghosts had allowed Scrooge to see himself as dead man.

"That was telt tae me by my uncle Charlie, and he ended up a dominie, a headmaster o' a fine school in Aberdeen, he never telt me a lie in his life." Didey said simply. We thought this was brilliant, that our grandfather had seen a ghost, and that there were ghosts in the village. At ten years old we couldn't understand why he wouldn't tell us more about the story. That day in front of the fire, sitting on our little stools, James and I, who knew each other inside out, had no idea that these stories which surrounded us growing up would be the very building blocks of our future. That story from Didey John was the beginning of all our stories.

CHAPTER 1

The wind howled mournfully around the house that evening, causing Annie and her sister Maggie to cuddle up together in the box-bed, while their boisterous brother Charlie was standing in front of the fire, acting out steering the wheel of some giant merchant ship. He was mimicking the sound of the wind and the waves, "Whoosh, splosh! And the waves are getting higher and higher, and they're coming in ower the ship! And the deck's getting soaked! But I'm bold Captain Duthie, a famous pirate, I can steer her round Cape Horn!" he narrated as his sisters looked at him incredulously.

"Charlie, you're feel! And you're making a noise, Mam will be mad at you!" Annie shrieked accusingly.

He ignored her and continued with his loud tale of adventure until his father James came in swiftly behind him and scooped him up in his arms. "Ah, but the waves can carry a man aff his feet, my boy, even on a grand ship! Ye must learn to respect the sea, Charlie, it is a chancy creature!"

"Dad! I didna hear ye come in! I was making up a story for Annie and Maggie, but they dinna like the storm!" Charlie explained, wrapping his arms around his father's neck as he was hoisted high in his arms.

"You're a fine storyteller, Charlie, and a very clever boy! I think one day you'll go to the College in Aberdeen and be a teacher, the sea gives too poor a living these days," James said ruefully.

"Oh no, I'm going to sea, I'm going to be a skipper, I'm going to be the best skipper in the whole of Buchan!" his green-eyed son replied.

James tousled his hair and put him back down on the ground. "It's as the Lord wills, Charlie." He turned to his girls, "Now you two fearties, why can you not be more like your brother? He isn't scared of the noise of the wind. It canna harm you here on the land, oh no!" James came and sat on the edge of the opening for the box bed which was situated against the central wall of their cottage, a rubble-built, lime-washed construction with a tiled roof. James could remember his grandfather telling him that they used to thatch the roofs, but tiles proved a sturdier alternative in spring storms.

"I dinna like the noise, it hurts my lugs!" Maggie cried, putting her hands over her ears to indicate her distress. She was the youngest and found it easier to elicit sympathy from her father than the rest of her siblings did.

"There is nothing to fear, my bonnie quine, there is a power greater than the storm, that can say to the waves 'be still,' and to the wind, 'cease blowing', and that is our Lord. When you say your prayers at night, you remember that and you'll not be feart," he assured.

"See? Ye shouldn't be feart, if the Lord is on our side!" Charlie chimed in and scrambled onto the bed with his sisters. "Dad, are ye going out tonight?" he asked in a quieter tone.

"Well, my lad, I hae to go, there's been sae few days we've managed to go tae sea lately that we have nae stores o' dry fish left, and your mam and your granny haven't been able to go to the country to sell ony fresh eens. The storm is blowing inland just noo, it might nae be so bad oot at sea, so we'll tak a chance and go oot just before dark. The glass is low, but it is moving up, the wind'll fare awa' by the morning. So you will be the man o' the house while I'm oot! Tak care o' yer mam and the little eens, especially this feartie here!" James reached his hand across and tousled his youngest daughter's brown hair. Maggie simply giggled.

"That I will, Dad, ye ken I will!" Charlie declared, striking his hand on his chest with pride.

Just then, their mother, Elizabeth Duthie, known to her neighbours as Betsy, came into the room from the "butt", the grander part of the cottage which, unlike the "ben" where all the cooking and dining took place, had a wooden floor and ceiling. The butt also contained a box bed where James and Betsy slept, and so too would their forthcoming child. Betsy's apron was now tight over her swollen belly, the baby due within a month. The children were delighted at the thought of a new brother or sister, but Charlie especially had added the request to his prayers every night since he had been told of this new arrival that it might be a boy, so he could have a brother to play with. Yes, he had his friends in the village, but it wasn't the same as a brother of his own!

"Now bairns, it's time you were getting yer night clothes on and getting tae bed! It'll be hard enough tae sleep wi' the wind, without you being wound up like a clock wi' Charlie's stories!" Betsy sounded tired. James stood up and put his arm around his wife's waist.

"Ach, dinna be hard on the boy, he's gaun tae be cleverer than us aa one day. Now, I'm awa' tae gie the boat a lookie o'er, then I'll be back for ma oilies and say cheerio," he said, gently drawing her to his side.

Betsy looked up at him, seeing the same green eyes as those of their son. Green like the sea filled with wrack, she had always thought, deep and gentle, the very aspect which had attracted her to him in the first instance. "Tak care, my dear, caul iron tae ye and the crew!" she said.

James squeezed her closer still. "And you, my dear quine, tak care o' the bairn that's to come, nae worrying aboot me! It's aye as the Lord wills." He kissed her cheek and with a few strides was out of the door. Betsy wiped her hands on her apron. She sighed. The ritual never changed, James went to sea, and she fretted at home, just as her mother had done over her father and brothers many decades before.

"Mam, what's cauld iron?" Annie asked, jumping off the bed onto the sand-strewn floor.

"Oh dear quinie, you a fisher and ye don't know that yet? Charlie, tell your sister what cauld iron means!" Betsy said in a mock-scolding tone.

"We daurna say 'good luck' when Dad goes to sea, so we say 'cauld iron' instead. Ye dinna say the name o' the red fish either, some folk call it cauld iron tae. It's because the evil spirits and witches are feart of iron, it keeps them awa' fae our boats when they're oot at sea! Didey Andrew telt me that. But he says we should aye pray to the Lord also!" Charlie explained. Betsy's father, Andrew Buchan was now in his seventies, but was still very much engaged in the business of the sea, whether repairing the nets of his sons and grandsons, or teaching them the coastal landmarks which either indicated rocks to be avoided, or good fishing to be taken advantage of. The old lore of the sea was what he believed protected the fleet – yet he was a regular at the little church hall in the centre of the village.

"My father aye said better to be friends wi baith Auld Hornie and the Almighty, since ye never knew who ye would be greeted by in the afterlife. We must never forget our traditions, Annie, that is what makes us fisherfolk different fae the landward folk, and sae it should always be! Now, time for bed, my dears, hap yer heids this night as the storm will be worse afore it gets better," Betsy told them. She hoped that the clasp knife in her apron pocket would be all the charm it promised against supernatural danger when her baby came.

"Cauld iron, safe against the storm!" Charlie declared triumphantly, also leaping onto the floor, darting across to the hearth and touching the iron grate. He hissed in pain, forgetting that the glowing embers made the grate too hot to touch. Betsy sighed. "Charles Duthie, jist behave yourself and get to bed! You're not too young to get the flat o' my hand on your dowp!" Charlie looked crestfallen, hearing his 'Sunday' name. He stepped quickly across to the door where one of their enamel water buckets stood and dipped his singed fingers into the cooling liquid. He shivered, but said nothing, turning back to his mother who presented him with his long, freshly-washed nightshirt. She smiled at him and shook her head, aye he was a clever one, but his boundless enthusiasm was wearing her out now.

"Come here, Charlie," she said tenderly.

Charlie flung his arms around her, and she enfolded him in her embrace. Whatever the future held, she knew she would never cease to be proud of her first-born child. He looked up at her, expectantly.

"Mam, I can hear the baby!"

"Aye? That's good. Now, off tae bed and say your prayers while I tie up the quines' hair." Betsy told him.

He squeezed her again, and whispered "Come soon, little brother, come soon!"

CHAPTER 2

J ames was satisfied that his little wooden fishing boat or yole was in order. He strode up from the windswept shingle shore to the village, a mere few yards, the fisherfolk having built their houses as close to their livelihood as they could, gable-end on to the ever-changing coastal waters. Two doors up from the Duthies lived one of James' two crewmates, Billy Stephen, a youth of eighteen, who was engaged to be married to James' cousin, Isabel, and thus family. Billy lived with his widowed mother, his duty since his older siblings had long left home. James rapped his knuckles on the sturdy wooden door and went inside, "Aye, Mrs Stephen, is yer boy ready for work?" he called.

Entering the "ben" living area, he saw old Mrs Stephen sitting in a large wooden rocking chair which was drawn up by the lively fire in the hearth. She wore a black bonnet fringed with lace and her dress was black too, as befitted a widow. The only colour variant came from her knitted shawl, which consisted of greys and blacks, stitched into traditional patterns which she would have had passed down to her by her own female relatives.

The black garb of fisher widows tended to make them look many years older than they actually were; Mrs Stephen was probably in her early sixties, her husband having been lost at sea seventeen years previously in a spring storm very much like the one raging over their heads this night.

"Hoo ye daen, young James? Billy's jist up in the laft seein' tae his lines, he'll be doon presently," the old woman spoke with a kindly tone. "How is Betsy wi' the bairn? It must be near her time?"

"Aye, it is that, maybe a month, maybe less. I just pray I'm nae at sea when it comes!" James replied, giving voice to his secret fear.

"Dinna worry, my lad, the howdie wife will tak care of her if ye are. And she has her sisters as weel! Are her feet cauld?" Mrs Stephen asked again.

James looked askance, then realised Mrs Stephen was trying to guess the child's gender with old folklore methods. He scratched his head, "Well, maybe aye, she didna used to want anything on her feet in bed, but she's knitted herself woollen moggans noo," he recalled Betsy purposefully knitting bed socks, or moggans as they were known locally, out of all her scraps of yarn not long after the "howdie" or unofficial midwife had agreed she was indeed expecting.

"Aye, ah-ha, and has she been cravin' for salty things? Sa'ted herrin' and the like?" Mrs Stephen grinned knowingly.

"Oh! Aye, she has, and Betsy said she aye hated salted herrin'! She taks it every week now, tae hersel', even if she disna mak it for us. So now, am I going to hae another daughter or a son according to that?" James smiled back, knowing he did not lay as much store by traditional beliefs as his wife and his fellow fishermen, but was kind enough to humour the older generation.

"Well it's a laddie; cauld feet, craving salt, a roon low belly all in front, ah-ha, that's fit the auld folkies aye said!" Mrs Stephen exclaimed triumphantly.

"Charlie will be pleased then, I've heard him at his prayers saying 'Dear Lord, please can I hae a brither this time?'!" James replied. Their conversation was interrupted by the sound of Billy's booted feet on the narrow wooden stair in the central closet of the cottage which connected the ground floor to the loft. His father had been a very successful skipper, so the

Stephens' cottage was a little larger than the others, with a distinct mending loft with an interior stair, as others tended to have their fishing gear hung up on the exposed beams of the "ben" or had an exterior stair into the floored part over the "butt".

"James! So we're goin'? I've jist made sure my hooks are a' in order," he explained, carrying under one arm his "skull" or shallow basket which held the single-stranded fishing lines. Each of the crew supplied their own lines which were played out into the sea as they spotted their catch, usually cod or haddock, and the big fish would gobble the mussel bait from the thousands of hooks attached to the lines at regular intervals. If the sea was choppy the lines would pull "fast" out of the basket and the crewmen would have be vigilant for hooks that snagged or breakages in the line.

"Aye, we must, if we get far enough oot we might avoid the storm. It's a typical March gale, right inland," James observed. "I'll go and chap on George's door, meet us doon at the shore, we winna dally."

"Righto, skipper," Billy smiled. He had freckles pitted across his nose, and fair hair, bleaching more every season he was

at sea, making him look hardly older than eight-year old Charlie.
Billy's bride to be was barely sixteen, but already well-versed in
the skills needed to be a fisherman's wife. "Cheerio, Mam, I'll be
back in the morn," he turned to his mother.

"Bless ye both, and cauld iron!" Mrs Stephen replied.

James and Billy parted at the door and James carried on up the
little street to his other crew member, George Bremner, who was
the husband of Betsy's sister Mary. Mary too was a fisher widow,
but having lost her husband at only twenty and having two
children to bring up, she soon married George, who although
now thirty-five years old, had never taken a wife before, and had
still lived with his aging parents. George and Mary now lived
next to the small village shop which was still open even at that
late hour. James gave a returning wave, seeing proprietor,
Kenneth Strachan raise his hand to him as he passed the window.

Again, as was his habit, James gave a knock before
entering the Bremners' abode. Mary was clearly having the same
trouble as Betsy in getting her children to settle during this wild
weather. Her twins, Andrew and Mary, were playing what

appeared to be a complex clapping game as their mother scolded them for still not putting on their night clothes. When she heard James, she turned and sighed, "Oh James, what am I to dae with these wee rascals? I've told them a dozen times tae get ready, but here, you see they're still up!"

"Maybe you should ask your father to come doon and tell them that the spirit o' the wind will carry them aff if they don't go to bed!" James chuckled, knowing his father-in-law's penchant for terrifying folk tales.

"Aye! Maybe I should! Are yours ony better?" Mary asked.

James shook his head and smiled, "Charlie was acting out being a sea captain and fearing the wits oot o his sisters when I left. It will take a' Betsy's patience to get them doon for the night!"

Mary was the same height as her younger sister, but dark rather than red-haired as was Betsy. She had the same bright blue eyes and freckles, yet was also less easy-going than Betsy. James' wife seemed better able to hide her fears. "Oh dear, I'll need tae help her when the new bairn comes! And are you nae foolish to risk yer lives goin oot in that big sea? Every other breaker I hear across the shore sounds closer than the een before!"

"James kens what he's daen, ma quine, that's why he's skipper!" It was George; tall, broad-shouldered with a wind-ravaged complexion, his black hair streaked with grey, he was an old hand at the fishing now. "So, ye've been in by Billy's?" James nodded, "Well then, I'll get ma lines and we'll gaun to the boat together. Though you've yer oilskins tae collect, aye?"

"I telt Betsy I would come back for them, see the bairns are beddit," James answered.

George put his arm around his wife's shoulder, and looked over at his step-children as they giggled and clapped their way through their rhymes. "Bairns! Bed-oh!" he exclaimed suddenly. Startled, Andrew and Mary instantly cuddled each other close, but when they saw it was their stepfather, they jumped to their feet, ran to George and wrapped their arms around his waist.

"Oh Faither, Faither, are ye goin out in the storm?" young Mary's tone was fearful.

"Beware if ye see the curly-tail or the lappy, Faither, ye ken they're bad luck!" Andrew chimed in.

"My dears, those chancy beasts winna be abroad in weather like this! And your uncle James is one o' the best skippers in the district, he'll get us tae the fishing grounds and back safe as weel!" George assured them, bending down to embrace them. Andrew turned to look at his uncle.

"Cauld iron, Uncle James, bring oor Faither back safe!" the little boy said, his fears perhaps rooted in the vague memories of his infancy when his natural father was lost.

"I will, but you must aye pray for our safety as weel, there's a time coming fan the charms and rituals of oor fathers winna help us. Your Didey Andra kens that, and he'd say it if he wis here. So, be good tae your Mither and awa' tae yer beds, and we'll be back aa the sooner!" James told his nephew, patting the eight-year-old on the head.

The twins gave George and Mary a cuddle each and went to climb into their box bed where they began to change into their night clothes. Mary kissed her husband's cheek, then reached behind her for the skull basket filled with George's fishing lines and presented them to him.

"I'll leave the lantern lowin' in the window till mornin', be sure and wake me if I'm nae already up," Mary said anxiously.

George said no more, knowing his wife's fearful nature, and turned to the door with the basket under his arm, following James outside. The two men found it hard going walking back against the wind to James' cottage. The wind seemed determined to whip the very skin from their faces such was its ferocity.

Betsy was already waiting at the door, her black woollen shawl wrapped around her head and shoulders as the sea spray in the wind dashed against the walls of the cottage.

"The bairns are finally in bed – whether they're asleep or nae, is another matter. I let Charlie sleep in our bed for peace, he'd only keep telling the quines stories otherwise," she said loudly over the storm. She saw her brother-in-law and hailed him, "George, how are the twins?"

"Hallirackit as ever! But I widna begrudge them onything!" He replied with pride.

James laughed, "Aye, he's too saft! Mary has a' the throwe-come wi them, and George gets tae be the favourite!"

"Ach, well, I canna help it, nae efter fit their mother's been through. But we better get yokit, the wind feels like it's turnin'," George observed.

Betsy had taken James' sea boots and oilskins to the door so he could don them there and then without needing to re-enter the house. He slapped the sou'wester cap on his head just as George finished speaking.

"Best get ahead o' it then, we'll need to go out by the Point and turn for Kinnaird Head before we go oot tae the grounds," James said, turning his head away from the blast as Betsy stood further inside. "Dinna bide there and catch cauld, I'll see ye the morn," he said softly, recognising the light of fear dancing in his wife's eyes. She felt another shiver of unease, but said no more. The two men walked off back down to the shore, as Betsy pulled fast the door behind her. Something gnawed inside her very soul that night, a fear stronger than ever. She could dismiss it as worry about the baby's condition in her womb, but no, it was a fear about James. Betsy had been brought up to observe all the folk rituals connected with safety since she had been a little girl, and although her parents also taught her to pray and read her Bible, the old ways seemed more deeply ingrained. James was so different; he appeared free of the clutch of what townsfolk would call superstition and ignorance. His faith was rooted in the Lord and he was the more peaceful for it.

Yet no amount of prayer would cast this unholy terror from Betsy's mind. There had been omens, but she tried to ignore them. There had been the huge black crow which had flown into the window, its wings spread wide as it hit the glass. Maggie had been with her at the time, but the little girl was only concerned about the bird's welfare, not knowing the import of such an occurrence. The bird of ill-luck had landed outside on the strip of grass by the door, but by the time Maggie reached it, the creature had recovered and stomped off rather indignantly. Then Betsy herself had seen a shooting star the previous night – she had told her father about that. Andrew Buchan had grimaced, and pronounced his verdict, "Well, ma quine, ye ken fit the auld folkies believed… the star falling from the heavens is a sign of a soul about to return to its Maker." She had omitted to explain that the star had appeared directly over their house. Clinging on to the hope that since all bad things came in threes, Betsy assured herself that she had not seen a third omen, so perhaps there was no disaster imminent.

She peeked in to the box bed where her daughters lay; they were now sleeping quietly, back-to-back with the blankets pulled up to their necks. Betsy was relieved, and carefully pulled the curtain across the open part of the wooden partition which formed the wall of the box. She stepped silently through to the butt to see if her son was still awake. When she entered the room, she saw the light from the candle which was set in the holder on the tiny corner ledge in the box bed. Charlie was sitting up with the blankets and sheets pulled around him, reading a book; it was *Kidnapped* by the popular Edinburgh writer, Robert Louis Stevenson.

Betsy watched him, his eyes scanned the page quickly, as if drinking in the words. "Charlie, you'll never sleep reading that! Yer father says it's nae mowse!" she whispered.

"Oh Mam! It's an affa good story! Ahm needin tae ken if Alan Breck will end up in the jile! Can I nae read tae the end o the chapter?" he begged. Betsy sighed again, she sat down heavily on the wooden chair next to the bed.

"Charlie, Charlie, you're jist a wee nickum!" her tone was affectionate, despite wanting to scold him, "Fit aboot if you read it to me? Jist tae the end o' the chapter like ye promised, then ye must try an' sleep. Ye hae school the morn, and though I'm sure your teacher wid be pleased that ye're enjoying Mr Stevenson's book so much, she'll tak ill at ye if ye're too tired tae work!" Charlie agreed readily and began to read to his mother, though not so loudly he might disturb his sisters.

James, Billy and George were now pulling the yole down to the water's edge. The wind was now blowing across their path from the north-east, causing George to remark again that it was changing direction. The shore here had a natural haven between many large coastal rocks. It was an ideal landing and launching site for the fishermen, and had been so as far back into antiquity as any man could recall. The old men reckoned that the hunter-gatherers of ancient times had come here to settle temporarily every summer when the white fish was plentiful around the coast.

Now all that concerned James as skipper was being able to navigate out to their usual fishing grounds, eight miles offshore in a gale which could blast them into Eternity on a whim.

As the boat began to float, the men climbed in and began to row, each yole having three sets of oars each. The tiny yoles had a single tall mast, were undecked and about twenty feet in length, yet they were broad, fast boats which suited the subsistence-fishing of that coast. The skull baskets were stored aft, ready to play the lines out. James kept an eye on the rudder, rowing with only one oar. They would not raise the sail until they were clear of the Point, a large rocky promontory which shielded the village from their neighbours in the town of Fraserburgh. Using the Kinnaird Head Lighthouse, which stood at the far side of the bay, James would be able to take a reading from his compass and they would go out into the open sea.

It was a struggle to row in the crosswind, but they were heartened to see others following them in their own boats. A few other desperate souls had decided to take the same risk to break the long spell of inactivity forced by the prevailing winds that month. The beacon which stood at the very tip of the Point on a rock called the Briggs was flickering wildly in the storm, but it signalled the time to turn left and head towards Fraserburgh. As the crew concentrated on the business of rowing hard, James began to pray silently; *Lord, keep us safe like You did Your disciples on the Sea of Galilee. Keep the waves from overwhelming us and bring us hame with the light o' day.*

CHAPTER 3

The wind had shifted into a more favourable position now, and the tiny fleet of yoles began to spread out in the fishing grounds known as Wast Shall, where haddock and codling often fed. There were various means to find the fish, even in the dark, but nearly all the fishermen from the village shared several lifetimes of experience between them, and knew the habits of their prey intimately. James knew of a secret "pot" in which the haddock liked to hide, thus that was the ground George rowed across as James held one basket after another as Billy played out the lines into the choppy water. It was a bitter, biting atmosphere, making Billy wonder if he had been better to take a nip of whisky before leaving the house, but he knew his mother would have smelt it on his breath. He could not wear gloves to do this job, so his fingers were soon stiff with cold, yet he continued, slapping one hand hard against his thigh to thaw his fingers as he pulled the lines with the other, then alternated and repeated the process. James could see he was struggling.

"We've nearly shot them a', Billy, ye'll soon be done!" the skipper called encouragingly.

"I hear ye, Skipper," the young man replied, his whole body shivering, despite the oilskins, the warm moleskin trousers and his fisherman's gansey underneath. "Fit wye do we carry on wi this, Skipper? Day in, day oot?" he added.

"Because it's who we are, Billy. We're fishermen, as were oor fathers, and their fathers, and so on into the mists o' time. The salt water runs in oor veins and we canna do anything else!" James replied proudly.

"We widna survive in a toonser or country job, Bill, we ken the sea, and that's that!" George roared over the spray, his face set grimly, his gloved hands clenched tightly around the oars.

"Last line, Billy, that's you lowsed now, pit your gloves on!" James told him as the twine slipped rapidly out of the basket on his lap. Billy gladly tossed the anchor rope to which was attached a marker buoy, into the boiling waves and the task was complete. James grabbed his crewmate's woollen mitts from the floor of the boat and shoved them quickly over Billy's frozen fingers.

"Thank you, Skipper, am I glad tae see the back o that! Fit a nicht, fan will it ever end?" he exclaimed.

"Oh Billy, surely yer Mither telt ye that this is "Hungry Mairch"? The prevailing winds are nearly aye onshore at this time o' year!" George retorted, as if irritated by the younger man's complaint.

Billy's bride-to-be, Isabel, James' cousin through his maternal uncle, Robert Lawrence, was far more concerned with her sister's health at that present time. Mary Lawrence was about to give birth, yet the father of her child was somewhere up in the Arctic Ocean on a whaling ship, utterly oblivious to the consequences of his dalliance with this wayward fishergirl. Mary had feared her parents' reactions, so had gone into hiding when first she had discovered her condition. She had told only her sister, who also knew where she was to be found.

Mary had gone to the "Gaun Aboot Folk", the Travellers, or gypsies as some called them. She knew that they were fairly tolerant of women having children out of wedlock and it was the Travellers that the howdie wives consulted for remedies and herbs to soothe the pains of birth. However, when the first waves of labour had jolted Mary's young body, she screamed for her sister, and one of the Traveller children went down to the village from their temporary campsite deep in the woods of Lord Saltoun's estate. The current owner, a shipping magnate called Mr Duthie, had been gracious enough to allow them to remain there during this stormy period.

The child, a barefooted girl of about twelve, wrapped in a sheepskin jerkin had appeared at the door of the Lawrences just as darkness fell. Isabel, already concerned about Mary being outside in such weather, had leapt up from her knitting by the fire and pulled the child inside. Having quickly established Mary was in need, Isabel hastily shoved her stockinged feet into her leather ankle boots and grabbed her brother John's old oilskin coat from the central closet of the cottage. Her mother was asleep in the ben, her father Robert and brothers were out at sea, needlessly risking their lives at the height of a storm, she thought. She queried why the child was wearing no shoes yet had a decent warm coat, to which the girl, wise beyond her years, replied "Ma

feet have been lang eesed tae the grun, dilly, am nae in need o'
beets!"

Isabel shook her head; she could not understand the
ability of these folk to cope with outdoor living, having only their
tents of canvas and hazel boughs for shelter, and yet the girl
strode ahead confidently in near darkness, as she herself struggled
to keep pace. They scrambled across the railway at the Philorth
Halt which bridged the stream from which it took its name.
Isabel could just see points of light through the trees, guessing
they were the lights in Cairnbulg Castle – Mr Duthie was known
to have plans to restore it to its former glory since the Frasers
had lost the estate many centuries previously.

Isabel followed the child into the wood along a path
which consisted of tiny stones that glowed eerily white in the inky
dark. Soon they were in a clearing where the camp was situated;
about a dozen hazel bough tents had been erected close together
and a huge bonfire dominated the centre of the circle. Isabel
immediately identified her sister's howls of agony as her guide led
her to the correct tent. The child ducked inside and Isabel heard
her talk in her own cant dialect, understanding little. She was

then beckoned inside and saw Mary, sitting astride a mound of horsehair blankets and makeshift pillows stuffed with chaff. Beads of nervous sweat trickled down Mary's face; her fringe was plastered to her forehead and she was flanked by two older Traveller women, both calling out encouraging instructions. Mary had her knees bent and a third woman, acting as midwife, knelt in front of her, peering into the intimate space between her legs.

"Isabel! Oh sister, am I grateful to all the powers of heaven and earth to see ye! The bairn is coming!" her voice rose to a shriek as another spasm of contraction shook her body.

"Mary! Looks like these wifies ken their business, what can I dae?" Isabel answered.

"Come here and hold ma hand, then Maria here can help Iona tae deliver the bairn!" Mary gasped. The Traveller called Maria nodded, "Aye, dilly, best she has family wi' her at this o' a' times! Ailsa here is a smart wee ranklie, she kent whaur you bade, telt us your Ma had given her a cuppie tay once, so she wisna feart to go to a scaldie hoose!"

Isabel was surprised that Isabel Lawrence Snr would ever have entertained a "tinker" child at the door, let alone given her something to drink. Perhaps her mother might be more forgiving of Mary than her youngest daughter imagined. She guessed the word "scaldie" meant non-Traveller; she'd heard it before, hissed angrily by Traveller laddies who had been chased away from the mussel beds at the village shore by the fishermen.

Soon, Mary was gripping Isabel's hand with enough ferocity to crush her fingers, but Iona the midwife said the time was coming nearer. Isabel was frightened; she had never seen a birth. She and her brothers had been sent across to their auntie Margaret's when Mary came. Her eldest brother, Arthur, had told her a horrible story about watching a lamb being born on a nearby farm. He had gone to ask for some chaff to fill the household mattresses, and the farmer had invited him to come and see the lambing.

"It was like a monstrous wet, bloody balloon with a baby sheep in it that came oot of the ewe's backside! The fairmer had tae pull it oot by its legs, he said ewes were feel and couldna gie birth withoot help. There were guts and dirt and blood everywhere! And the ewe licked its bairn clean with her ain tongue!" Arthur had enjoyed seeing Isabel's disgusted expression, and added more gruesome detail about the smells and sounds of the animal birth. Now, as a sixteen year-old about to get married, watching her fifteen year-old sister produce a baby, she was shaking in fear at the thought of what would come from Mary's body.

"Now, ma bonny dilly, I can feel the bairn's head, it'll be here in a wink, jist push as hard down onto yer bottom as ye can!" Iona instructed cheerfully. She had her jet black hair tied back in a colourful Paisley headsquare, yet the bright gold hoops in her ears glinted in the light of the several lanterns inside the tent. She had the sleeves of the grey blouse she wore rolled up to her elbows, a clean white cotton cloth across her lap, and a large bucket of steaming water by her side in which floated a sea sponge. Isabel could not think what was coming. Mary yowled like a scalded cat as she pushed with all her remaining strength. The other women whooped and cried out encouragement as suddenly a tiny, blood-spattered head appeared to slip into Iona's weathered hands.

"That's the wye! Eence mair, dilly, nearly there!" she exclaimed.

"If I see that whaler again, I'll KILL him!" Mary shrieked as she gave the final heave. At last the pain eased, the awful stretching, tearing feeling stopped. Iona held a baby in her arms.

"Mary! Mary! Oh look!" Isabel cried. "What is it?" she enquired of Iona, as she took the sponge from the bucket and wiped the blood, membrane and moisture from the baby's skin.

"First time ye've seen a bairn being born, eh? Well, you're now aunt to a bonny wee girlie!" Iona grinned, displaying a set of pearly white teeth. "Now, my braw, brave dilly, best the bairn meet her Nesmore, while we clean ye up," she continued, having wrapped the baby in the cotton cloth and placed her gently onto Mary's chest, and placed the new mother's arms around her.

Isabel then saw a large red, lumpy substance in a pool of blood on the rush mat floor of the tent by Mary's feet. "Oh govey dicks! Fit's that?" she gasped.

Maria laughed uproariously, "Aye, aye, dilly dream we hae here! It's the afterbirth, the stuff that the baby's been sustained by a' these months. We folk will bury it here in the camp and it will dae the land good. There's some Irish I've heard o even eat them!" Isabel wrinkled her nose, and wondered if they were teasing her for her innocence. "Every deem that gies birth casts the birth bag after the bairn, and has done since Eve, the Mither of all living!" Maria added.

"Now, there is something you can do as the bairn's nearest kin present, a task the faither should dae, but we ken Mary's story, aye, you can cut the birth cord, the final act to bring the bairn into this world," Iona told her, having restored Mary's dignity somewhat and bade her ease her legs down onto the blankets.

"Oh! Aye, we are nae likely to see the nyaff that put Mary in the family way again, so I will dae it, tell me how!" Isabel replied excitedly. Iona produced what looked like a gutting knife, its blade sharp and bright. She handed it to Isabel and bade her wait a moment as she tied two lengths of twine around the cord to seal off the blood supply. It was just then Isabel became aware of the storm again; the tent had been a secluded haven for the last half hour or so, but now the wind squealed through the trees and rain swooshed through the still-empty branches.

Iona held the cord either side of her tourniquets, "Now, cut it through, one stroke if ye can, but nae mair than three!" she instructed.

Isabel felt her heart thudding beneath her ribs, but she tried to steady her hand. Just think o' slicing the heid aff a giant cod fish, just dae it! she told herself. She raised the knife and struck down strongly, and with more ease than it took to part the head from a cod, the skin of the cord broke in two. "Well done, dilly, the bairn is now part of the world of man," Iona pronounced.

Mary looked up at her sister, beaming with joy. "Thank you so much, Isabel, for everything…" she said.

"Ye've your wee tinker friend to thank for risking hersel' coming across the railway in pitch dark tae the village! But no, I wid never leave ye. I think our Mam might be right gled tae ken ye're safe and sound, let me tell her, please?" Isabel begged.

"Oh Isabel, I canna, nae now, nae when there's a bairn as weel! And Faither will slay me! No, better I bide awa' here wi' good friends that dinna cast the first stone o' judgement," Mary sighed.

Isabel looked at the baby properly for the first time. Her round head had a few tufts of ash blonde across her scalp. She had surely inherited her father's hair colour; none of their family were so fair. But the baby's eyes, a deep sea-green were a Lawrence trait indeed. Their father and brothers all had green eyes, as did their cousin James and his boy Charlie. She was so tiny! She had yelped like a fractious puppy dog when she had made her entrance, but was now breathing gently, the anxiousness of seizing life gone. The child was perfect as far as Isabel could see, a miracle of creation, right enough, just as another young girl called Mary had experienced many centuries before them in a faraway country.

"What will ye name her?" Isabel asked.

Mary looked back at her daughter. "Well... I think she should be Isabel Iona Lawrence, after her auntie and her midwife!"

Iona, Maria, their friend Flora and the little Traveller girl, Ailsa, standing around them in a protective huddle, burst into gleeful laughter. Maria clapped Iona's shoulder, "And mony's the mither that Iona's helped has daen likewise!"

"Bless ye, dilly, you'll be a kind and patient mither, that I can see!" Iona said with the air of a prophet. The women began to sing in their own tongue and others gathered outside the tent, guessing the child had been safely delivered. Many a blessing was heaped on little Isabel-Iona that stormy night, that her aunt almost forgot about Billy out at sea.

Out in the Wast Shall, James Duthie saw one of their neighbour boats drawing alongside, their skipper holding aloft his lantern; it was his Uncle Robert, and cousins, John and Arthur Lawrence.

"James! Are ye bidin' oot? The storm's turnin' this direction, it's time we were awa' hame. We've already pulled oor lines, naethin but a few stray codlings!" Robert called.

"Ach, ye're right, it's the poorest nicht I've seen this while!" James shouted back over the noise of the wind. "We'll see ye at Belger shore, I needna tell ye tae be careful, because ye will. The Lord protect ye, Rob," he added.

"And tae yersels," Robert replied, and his sons began to row, fearing to raise their sail as the wind seemed to be turning every direction of the compass at that moment.

"Come on, boys, let's get those lines in, we've been o'er the Green Pottie, there's a good chance we micht even scrape a bag's worth o' haddies!" James encouraged. This time, Billy rowed back across the area they had cast their lines, and George hauled in the buoy and anchor rope, then pulled the twine carefully, winding it into the skulls, hoping to find a fish to deposit in the tiny hold at the bow of the boat. James began to row too, seeing his cousin's fiancé making little progress. He suspected that Billy spent too much time at the "Inn", the only licensed ale house in the village. The fisherfolk had been strong advocates of Temperance for a generation due to the combination of Salvation Army evangelical campaigns and the protests of the irate wives and mothers of fishermen who had wasted their meagre living at the taverns and pubs of Fraserburgh. The Inn was the last refuge for those who could not or would not take "the Pledge", run by Mrs Jean Carle, née Fyfe, an old woman who had originally come from the country, her father a farmer, to marry John Carle, one of the first men to go to the whaling from their village. The whalers were bold drinkers, encouraged by their fellow seafarers from Shetland and

Newfoundland with whom they travelled to the distant icy waters of the Arctic North. Jean very much enjoyed the money she made, but her neighbours were increasingly hostile towards her, believing her in league with the Devil, such was their hatred of drink. James found it hard enough that the old widow refused to stop supplying ale and whisky, but harder when Jean Carle was his maternal great aunt. She despised her sister's in-laws for being "kirk greedy" as she called it. James had given up trying to reason with her, but continued to pray that the old woman's heart would be softened one day to see the desperate straits that the families of alcoholics were in and give up her licence.

As far as Billy's lack of strength and contrary attitude was concerned, James tried to protect him from George's impatience, but encouraged him to work hard. "Billy, come away, laddie, it'll be daylight afore we get these lines in!" he shouted, trying to sound cheerful.

"I am, Skipper, I am, but the wind's in ma face, my arms are sair!" Billy groaned.

"Naethin hard work winna cure, Bill, we've the last skull o lines tae collect, so pit some effort intae it!" George retorted.

"Skipper, we've got a half-a-dozen haddies, two codlings, the line feels light, ahm nae sure that we'll get much mair!" he turned to James who was rowing furiously to make up for Billy's inattention.

"We'll hoist the sail efter this, once we've turned inshore, the wind'll blast us back hame wi' a' speed!" James told them. George nodded his approval. His suspicion about the lack of catch on the remaining hooks was proved correct as only one more solitary haddock flopped into his lap. He took the hook from its mouth and banged its head hard on the side of the boat to stun it, then he dropped it into the basket stowed tight under a few boards at the helm.

The three men then took up oars and rowed hard against the boiling waves to pull out of the wind and turn the yole towards the shore. James pulled his compass out of his pocket, held it by the lantern which was now set by his feet and saw they were pointing south. "Good, now, unlatch the sail and pull her up," he ordered.

The tiny boat tossed like a cork in a vast bucket as Billy and George began the business of untying and hoisting their sail up the mast, which had been creaking suspiciously as the force of the air might snap it in half at any moment. He had ignored George's earlier comment about "whistling masts" — to whistle at sea was taboo, but especially during a storm such as this. The fishermen feared when the eerie sound emanated from any part of their craft, as it was a perceived sign of disaster.

Billy appeared to have recovered some energy and hauled the ropes to which the sail was attached. The red sailcloth billowed out like a blossoming spring flower until it was stretched tight. George finally fastened the large iron hook on the end of the sail to the bow. The little yole surged forward, slicing into the breakers, and James attended the tiller. The sea heaved beneath them as if some marine leviathan was tossing the boat up with its fishy bulk. The spray was made worse as hail began to lash their backs. James resumed his silent prayers, knowing this was the fiercest gale he had ever encountered in his sixteen years at sea. The mast creaked and squealed violently. James was thrown hard into the starboard side of the yole. He gasped as the hard timber connected with a rib; Lord, keep my bones as you did those of your Son, let none be broken! He prayed fervently.

"James! That was an unco knock ye got, are ye fit?" George called out. James just nodded and smiled through gritted teeth.

"I dinna like the sound o' that creaking, Skipper, will she hold?" Billy observed gloomily.

"She'll hold. I built this boat wi' my father ten years ago, she's sound as a bell!" James retorted.

Suddenly the sky was encompassed by a vivid flash of white followed by a heavy peal of thunder. Billy let out an unmanly scream. James seized the tiller again, to keep their path steady. George joined him. A few seconds later there was another flash and this time a bang like canonfire. Billy looked up, "The mast's on fire! The lightning struck it! In Neptune's name fit will we dae?"

The sailcloth was quickly alight. If it reached them the boat would catch fire too, even in this world of water. Billy saw James say something into George's ear, and he clambered forward, unloosed the rope. "Billy, get yer heid oot o the road! Lie doon!" the older man roared. Billy did as he was bid without further argument and cowered in the bow along with the fish basket. The sail flapped loose; George took his gutting knife and slashed the ropes which tethered the sail to the mast. As he cut desperately at the hemp, the wind whipped at the loose cloth like greedy fingers; the last slash of the blade and the sail was torn away into the spray-filled night.

"Why did ye dae that, George? We're surely gaun to be smashed to smithereens on the rocks withoot a sail!" Billy wailed.

"Because the skipper telt me to! Stop bein sic a feartie and pick up yer oars!" George shouted back at him.

James saw their distress and leaned towards them, picking the lantern up and holding it close by his face so they could see him. "Boys, boys, listen tae me, we are nae going to get through this nicht picking fault wi' each other! Now, you must tell me this, are baith of ye ready tae enter Eternity?" his tone was solemn.

Billy grabbed George's arm; they looked at each other. Billy knew he was far away from believing anything these days, he trusted the bottle more than any prayer to get him through, and yet if he died tonight he would leave his mother, his bride to be, his sisters and brother, never to see them again, his future uncertain. George feared leaving Mary and the twins; she had already lost one man. George had given little thought to God, hoping his morals and forbearance were enough to please others. "James, you ken the truth, we are baith careless men who have paid nae heed to the things of the soul! I am nae ready to meet my Maker, nae now as it stands, and Billy here is just a bairn wi much tae learn!" George eventually said.

"Well, I am, I ken my end, that I will meet my Saviour at the Mercy-seat of Grace that the Prophet John saw in Revelation. My dear brither fishermen, kinsmen tae, let me get ye hame safe, and the Lord and I will ride oot the tempest!" James replied. They could see his eyes were glassy with emotion in the light of the lantern's flame. George had no doubts of his skipper's sincerity.

"James, div ye ken what yer saying? Fit will we tell Betsy? And yer mither and faither? They'll never forgive us if we come hame and you dinna!" George gasped, finding the words stick in his throat. James reached out his hand and grasped George's arm.

"Aye, yes, I do that! But dinna fret for them, they ken me, and if they thought the Lord took me and gave you the chance tae mak yersels richt wi Him, they would gie thanks and nae blame ye! Jist dinna waste anither minute, boys, leave the auld wyes behind. Superstition will never save ye, "cauld iron" disna hae the power o'er death! Promise me ye will repent!" he exclaimed, the words being whipped away by the wind, the boat whirling and tossing around at its mercy.

"Oh James, James, I will, I will, I'll gie up the drink, I'll be sober for ma weddin', but please, dinna spik aboot death, you're comin' hame wi us!" Billy began to weep, and grabbed James' arm.

"Have I not aye said it's as the Lord wills?" James assured him. The three men hugged each other. Without another word, George and Billy huddled in the bow; James took up the anchor rope of their fishing lines, looped it around his waist and the tiller, and tied it. Pulling a pair of oars towards him, he settled back and began to row. Every deed of his whole life flitted through his mind's eye; learning to braid nets with his father, his mother teaching him to cook soup, his first sight of his beloved

Betsy, and his children. Charlie would cope, he would be the man, the Lord would give him strength to keep the family going. But then, what about the baby would he guessed now he would never see?

Oh Lord, this is a hard journey You're takin' me, gie me the strength tae get these sinners back to the shore, but if You require my soul this nicht, then give me one answer tae prayer now, let me say goodbye to those I love best. The soul is made of immortal stuff, so take me tae my beloved Belger shorie, up tae my hoose, and in tae see my bairns and my wife eence mair, so let it be, Lord, so let it be! James prayed, sorrowful tears beginning to trickle down his rain-lashed cheeks. He began to sing his favourite hymn as loudly and lustily as he could.

"Will your anchor hold in the storms of life?/ When the clouds unfold their wings of strife?/ When the strong tides lift and the cables strain/ Will your anchor hold or firm remain?"

CHAPTER 4

Andrew Cardno had found it nearly impossible to sleep as the wind howled and whistled around the village all night. He lived in the second row of houses up from the shore, his cottage was diagonally across from the shop and Mrs Carle's infamous drinking establishment. His wife had scolded him for his tossing and turning. Andrew was annoyed; had he not bowed to her pleas to stay at home that night and not risk the tumult? Near dawn he decided to go and check his boat, fearing that it may have been damaged. The wind had died away to a whisper, the first streaks of watery daylight were beginning to glow out on the horizon as Andrew trudged down to the shore. The only sound now was that of the fisherman's boots crunching on the shingle. He guessed that it would be fully light before any of the fleet made it back from the likes of Wast Shall and Dusky, the favourite grounds of the fleet, thus is was a surprise when he caught sight of a distant figure leaning over one of the up-turned yoles. Surely one of his other neighbours had also stayed at home and had taken it into his head to ensure that his craft was intact. As Andrew got closer he recognised James Duthie, and waved in the semi-darkness to attract his attention. James waved back.

Andrew was keen to talk to him, as he was sure he had seen his neighbour and crew take their yole out yesterday evening. What had changed his mind? Quickening his pace, he eventually reached the boats and was practically face to face with James. He was looking straight ahead and suddenly James was no longer there. He walked up to the boat James had been leaning on, and recognised from the coloured stripe painted around the rim that it was not his boat, but that of Andrew's next-door neighbour, William Watt. James had disappeared. Andrew felt his heart begin to thud fast in his chest; to see a man when he should be at sea and then witness him vanish before one's very eyes meant only one thing — it was not James, but his wraith. Even in this enlightened age, fishermen feared the sight of such a thing; it was a sign that the person seen was about to die. James had gone out to sea in that terrible storm, and now he might not be coming back. Andrew steadied himself on the keel of the Watt yole, feeling that he was shaking with terror. He could not stay here, he had to go home, get indoors away from that unearthly vision. He turned and began to run up the shingle and then along the shore road. He saw the outline of the cottage belonging to James' parents, Charles and Margaret Duthie; it stood right on the corner of the village, the houses across from it being part of the neighbouring village of Inverallochy. The two were separated only by a tiny stream running down the main pathway to the sea. The stream, named the Stripey, flowed in a little stone-lined trough that the fishermen had built to stop it flooding the area on which people walked. It drained down into a natural channel just at the butt of the Duthie's. Andrew could hear it bubbling along rapidly, swollen by the rainwater of the previous night. He turned past the house and then stopped, finding himself in front of James and Betsy's door. Andrew knew he should tell Betsy, but then, how could he? The woman was expecting her next child imminently, a shock such as this could hurt the baby. And she was on her own with her children. He could not be so heartless, someone else would have to do it when the terrible thing had come to pass. He was about to continue on his way when Betsy opened the door.

"Andra! I thought it was James. I heard his sea-boots on the floor. Are they back yet?" she asked, looking very tired. He could hardly bear to look at her. "Eh… no, nane o' the fleet are back. I jist went tae see my boat wisna damaged… Alice widna hear o' me goin' t'sea yesterday," he said quickly, and went on his way, swallowing hard, wondering whether Betsy had been given a sign too, or if she was up early through natural concern, like any fisher wife. He shook his head, he could not have told her, no, not he.

Betsy closed the door. She felt that Andrew had been strange, as if he did not want to talk. Yet she and her son had heard the sounds of the door opening, hard breathing as if James had been running, and the clump-clump noise as his sea-boots were deposited on the floor. Charlie had said, "Dad's takin' an affa lang time to come through, maybe he's gone back oot again!" Betsy thought, yes, he's probably gone to relieve himself! She had gone out and walked around the cottage, but there was no sign of anyone, and when she returned to the door she could see there were no boots, no oilskin coat, indeed none of James' possessions that supported the evidence of the sounds mother and child had heard.

It was then Andrew had walked past, and she had hailed him. She felt a wave of nausea sweep over her; it wasn't just the baby, this was the third omen she had been dreading! How often had she heard her grandmother, Jeannie Brucie tell her stories of queer sounds and signs which presaged the death of someone in the house. Knocking, banging, a cold air where the loved one sat. And had she not herself seen the crow hit the window, the star fall from the sky and now hear the distinct noises her husband usually made when he entered the house? The charm was complete, three signs, and now Andrew's inexplicable reluctance to talk to her, something was very wrong and she felt it in the depths of her heart. Betsy walked back into the butt; Charlie was asleep again. What would he do without a father?

Out at sea the little yole was tossed back and forth. The storm had blown itself out. Suddenly the craft foundered; Billy Stephen and George Bremner thought at last they had reached the Cairnbulg shore. Both stiff and cold from the cramped position they had maintained throughout the night, the two men clambered up from the stern. Billy turned around and saw that James was gone. "James! No, no, no, James, far are ye?" the young man shrieked. "That last big lump o' water that hit us, it must hae taken him!" he leapt out of the boat and into the sea. George just stood, dumbfounded.

He realised that Billy had started wading out to see if he could see their skipper. Billy was shouting himself hoarse, splashing about in the water, hoping he might even find James unconscious, but then he felt George's hand on his arm. "Dinna shout ony mair, Billy. He's awa'. He said it himsel', he wis ready tae go. He kennt we needed mair time." George gulped back the lump in his throat; he had to show himself strong to the young man. Billy began to weep pitifully. George put his arm around his shoulders. "Weep only for yersel, Billy, laddie, James is in the heavenly realms, and pleading your case wi' his Lord. A' you can do is mak' good your promise tae gi'e up the drink and be a good man tae Isabel," he said gravely, knowing he had to put his spiritual affairs in order too.

Some of the rest of the fleet were now pulling into the shore. Robert Lawrence was the first to spot the two men standing by the battered yole. He guessed immediately what had happened. His nephew was lost. He and his sons quickly leapt out of their boat and pulled it high up the shore, as near as the grassy bents which fringed the dusty pathway by the houses. He then ran over to George and Billy. George saw him and shook his head.

"What happened?" Robert asked.

"He saved oor lives, Rob," George began. "I heard him praying and singing above the storm. He's awa'."

Robert stepped forward and clapped Billy's shoulder as the young man's body shook with his uproarious weeping. "Aye. James is with the Lord, nae one man in this village will doubt it." He sighed, feeling the pain in his heart, knowing his sister Margaret would be devastated. Now who would tell them?

Just then a number of schoolboys came running down to the shore as usual, all willing to help pull the boats up and maybe get a penny reward if the men were feeling generous. Willie Watt Jnr, whose father had stayed at home that night, was first in the throng. He was eleven years old and desperate to leave school and become a fisherman proper. He knew all the men in the fleet. He could see Arthur Lawrence looking downcast and ran up to his admired elder friend.

"Arthur, fit's adee? It wis an affa night, wis there men lost?" he enquired.

Arthur looked at him, knowing that in a year he too would be risking his life out on the ever-changing waters of the North Sea. "My cousin James Duthie. His crew came back, but they said he wis lost o'er the side. He wis tryin' tae row them hame safely," Arthur looked over Willie's shoulder, and to his horror saw little Charlie Duthie, running down from his house. "Bide a minute, Willie, there's my cousin's boy, I need tae tell him before onybody else does!" Arthur's father had also seen Charlie and they both met him at the same time. Robert bent down to address his great-nephew.

"Charlie, is yer Mam at hame?" he asked, trying to steady his voice.

"Aye she is, she's jist getting Annie ready for school. Uncle Robert, ye look sad, has something happened tae ma Dad?" Robert shivered at the boy's perception.

"Charlie, I need ye tae be brave, yer Dad is nae coming hame, he's been lost oot at sea," Robert said quietly. Charlie stared incredulously.

"Nah, nah, am nae believin' ye, Uncle Robert, far are Billy and George?" He ran past his relatives and straight for the edge of the shore where he recognised his father's yole. Even as he approached, he saw the broken mast, the cracked sides and the remains of the torn sail where George had cut it away.

"George, far's ma Dad?" Charlie asked, feeling a strange sensation well up inside him, like fear and sadness together. Billy saw the boy and quickly wiped his tears away, but Charlie could see that his eyes were red and swollen. George gasped, no, how can we tell him like this? But it was Billy who spoke as Charlie reached them.

"Charlie, yer Dad has gone tae Heaven, he told us we needed tae stay behind and mak ourselves richt wi the Lord. He saved oor lives, and the Lord's taken him hame tae the bright shore o Paradise," Billy said, crouching down to Charlie's level, the tears springing to his eyes again. Charlie looked up at George who nodded, and added, "Laddie, yer Dad wis the best Christian man I ever kennt, but he is gone."

"Gone? Lost? But I prayed he and you would a' be safe, why did the Lord nae answer my prayer? Why did He take my Dad?" The horrible feeling in his chest radiated out to his arms, his legs, his head, a pain like he had never experienced before. He flung his arms around Billy and screamed. Billy thought his own heart would break. Never would he go to sea again and put his bride and future family through such agony, there had to be a better alternative than dicing with death to pay for one's daily bread.

By this time, Arthur's younger brother, John Lawrence had gone up to Betsy's and knocked on the door. When she answered it and saw her husband's cousin, she knew the worst had come to pass.

"John, is he...?" she began.

"Oh Betsy, I'm so sorry, Billy and George said he saved their lives. He's gone!" John exclaimed.

Betsy felt everything spinning and a great pain in her belly. John saw she was about to faint, and slipped his arm around her to keep her on her feet. "Betsy, ye need tae sit doon, the men will be comin' up noo," he said, taking her inside. Annie and Maggie saw their father's cousin and skipped up behind him as he helped their mother get to the wooden rocking chair by the hearth.

"Cousin John, cousin John, is Mam nae well?" Annie asked.

"I don't know, Annie, dearie, yer brother will be coming back in a whiley, jist be good and watch yer sister," he replied, as lightly as he could, knowing that six year old Annie might find it hard to understand her father's absence, little Maggie even more so.

Robert, George and Billy came in, Billy carrying Charlie on his shoulders. Robert was relieved that his son had reached the cottage before them and delivered the terrible news. Betsy pulled her shawl around her shoulders, but when she saw Charlie, she opened her arms; Billy let him down onto the floor and he ran to his mother, wrapping his arms around her neck. He was weeping. She held him close, knowing that her fear and sorrow had to be hidden from him and the girls.

"I guessed, I guessed he'd been taen. Andra Cardno walked past this door jist at daylight and hardly said two words tae me, I think he saw something. I felt it, I've felt it comin' for days, so nae blamin' yersels, James was a believer in God, I ken he will be in Heaven now. Did ye see him go?" Betsy said quickly, taking deep breaths to keep back her tears.

"No. The mast was struck by lightning sometime in the nicht and the sail went on fire, James telt me tae cut it loose, then he telt us he would get us hame safely. He tied himsel tae the tiller wi the anchor rope and rowed alane. We felt the boat founder on the rocks efter a great lump o' water hit us, it could've been then, it could've been earlier, we jist dinna ken, as he bade us bourrachie up in the bow," George explained, his voice rough with emotion.

Billy was still wiping his tears away, "That's nae a' George, tell her the truth!" he exclaimed.

"Go on, Billy, fit did James say?" Betsy enquired, seeing his swollen eyes.

"He asked us if we were ready tae enter Eternity! We baith said we were nae, and the next thing he said wis that he kennt his end, and that it wis as the Lord willed! I heard him praying for us. He kennt the Lord wis gaun tae tak him hame, he said he was gaun tae meet his Saviour!" Billy cried, "I promised him I wid mak things richt, sae did George, we've been given anither chance, and it was James that saved us!"

Betsy looked at him, the fear and guilt in his eyes. That sounded just like James; he prayed for the family, he prayed for the crew, he was never done reminding folk ever so gently of the need to be right with the Lord. She felt hurt that her own superstitious nature had done much to erode her trust in the God of the Bible, that she had not been able to give up her need to control life with her own hands. It was a lesson to her too. They had all been granted another day, another chance to make sure their salvation.

"Billy Stephen, you keep that promise! I ken you've been daen things you widna want yer mither tae ken, and that Isabel's been worried aboot ye, now, ye've been telt! James never did onything in vain, so dinna let his last act on earth be! I'm nae mad at ye, but I will be if ye dinna mend your wyes. Now, awa hame and tell yer mither ye're still here, then see Isabel!" Betsy scolded.

Billy understood that kindness was at the heart of her admonishment, and left the cottage. George and Robert sat down both on the wooden bench by their table, neither daring to sit on James' armchair which was opposite Betsy. John had taken Annie and Maggie back to his mother's house.

"Ye'll need tae go next door and tell his folks. It will br'ak their hearts tae hear this," Betsy said.

Robert got up again, "I'll see them, Margaret is my eldest sister efter a'." he commented.

"Thank you, Robert, and wid ye go by my folks and tell them?" Betsy added, unsure if any of her brothers or cousins would have been able to tell them yet. Robert nodded and left.

Charlie looked up, having worn himself out. "Can I go tae Didey Duthie's an' a'? I dinna want him tae be sad," he whispered.

"Oh, bless ye, bairn, of course ye can," Betsy felt the tears finally spring to her eyes. Charlie clambered down off the rocking chair and ran after Robert.

"I can see James in him, ye ken," George remarked.

"Aye, he's a Duthie tae the core," Betsy replied, wiping her face with her apron. "George, did James really say he kennt his end? It sounds like him, but, I hae tae tell ye, I've seen two omens in the last few weeks, and this morning, fan I spoke tae Andra, baith Charlie and I were sure we heard James come in and tak his boots aff. I ken these are aa things that James laid nae store by, but it is what I wis brought up wi', I couldna help thinkin' the worst, and there's Billy sayin' that James kent it wis his time!" she explained, "Now, could it be that the Lord Himsel kent I needed the old signs, yet James had foreknowledge directly through his prayers?"

George looked at her, guessing she was trying to make sense of it all. He sighed and scratched his head, "I canna say, I am in as much need o' reforming my beliefs as ye are yersel', but there wis something... I never said tae Billy, it wid fear him, but jist fan that last wave hit us, I looked oot aft. There wis nae

James then, but a bricht, glowin' licht, like the moon had come doon intae the boat, and I jist felt this calm come o'er me. James wis awa', but tae a better place than this. I tell ye, it made me pray there and then! I begged the Lord tae get us back tae mak good oor promises. Maybe, maybe the Lord is ahint a' the things oor faithers and grandfaithers telt us, and if there was a wye for James tae mak his presence kent in the hoose eence mair afore he left this scene o' time, it wid hae certainly been the Lord's will , and nae the auld religion o' magic and mystery. Dinna tell a soul I said this tae ye, but tak' heart ma quine, yer man gave his life for us sinful feels left ahint, jist like the Lord Himsel'. If He took James, He'll gie you strength tae go on," he reached forward and patted his sister-in-law's hand.

Betsy felt the pains in her belly again, the baby had felt the shock; she only hoped that labour would not come early as a result. She needed to be on her own for that moment. "George, bless ye for tellin' me that. You get awa hame tae Mary, cos surely the bairns will have been tae school and heard by now, and she'll be worried. Annie and Jane will be here or lang syne, they aye come the day tae help me change the sheets, they'll look efter me," she told him, referring to her other sisters.

"Oh! Oh aye, Mary wis in a richt steer last nicht. I'll come back later, I'll hae a look at the boat, we'll need tae get it repaired," he said, rising from the bench.

"Nivver mind the boat, it'll bide far it is, awa and see yer wife!" Betsy encouraged.

She was relieved when he was gone. She got up and shut the door. A stabbing pain shot through her belly again. "No, please dinna come yet, I need tae go tae collect Maggie, please dinna," she gasped, leaning against the lime-washed interior wall.

CHAPTER 5

Isabel Lawrence had left her sister and new-born niece at the Travellers' camp in Lord Saltoun's wood, unable to persuade her to return to the village. It had been getting light as she made her way back across the railway line and followed it home. She reached the family house just as her brother Arthur came in the opposite direction up from the shore. He bore an expression of sadness which immediately struck Isabel to the heart.

"Oh no, not Billy!" she gasped.

Arthur held up his hand, "Billy's safe. It wis cousin James, he wis lost trying tae row the yole back. They are at Betsy's hoose jist noo," he explained quietly.

"Oh, oh no, and Betsy's expectin', oh this is terrible!" Isabel said, thinking of Mary's traumas the previous night.

"Aye. The storm was jist uncanny, we were a' sure somebody wid be taen. We spoke tae them at the fishing grounds; James wis jist turning for hame then. Nane o the fleet could see each other, there wis little we could hae done," Arthur muttered, his sou'wester in hand. Just then, their brother John came up behind them, holding the two little girls Maggie and Annie by the hand.

Isabel looked at her young relatives; they seemed oblivious to the situation. Annie might understand, they would have to explain to her, but the youngest, it was beyond Maggie's comprehension at four years old. "Far's Charlie?" she asked.

"Doon at the shore, ye ken he aye goes tae see Dad come back," Annie informed her brightly.

"Aye, I think he will be hame now, or either at yer Dide's hoose. Come in and see yer grand-aunt Isabel, she'll be pleased o the visit," Isabel said, beckoning them after her. The two girls let go John's hands and scuttled after their cousin.

"Isabel looks like she's been oot a' nicht. Div ye think she kens far Mary is?" Arthur commented to his brother.

"I dinna ken, but some good news wid help this day. I've twice seen een o' the tinker bairns in the village, maybe Mary is wi them, ye ken she is aye kindly tae them," John replied. "We better tell Mither then, Isabel will be keepin the bairns occupied."

Inside their cottage, Isabel Lawrence Snr was carrying Maggie up in her arms, a look of puzzlement on her face. The boys looked at their mother, and Arthur spoke, "James is lost. Dad's at theirs jist now." The flat tone of his voice convinced Isabel Snr that there was no question of her husband's nephew being found. She held the child close to her, trying hard not to show her sorrow.

"Maggie, I'm goin' tae the country today tae sell my fish, would ye like tae come and meet the fairmers and toffs?" Isabel said to the child, who was waving the little wooden toy boat she held up and down in the air, mimicking the motion of the waves.

"Ooh! Aye, please may I, grand-aunt Isabel? Mam will never take me, she says it's too far!" Maggie squealed with delight.

"Ah, but I can carry ye some o' the wye. And ye never ken, there are lots o horsies on the farms, ye may get tae ride on een!" Isabel told her, marvelling at the innocence of childhood, having long forgotten what her own children had been like in their youth. "And now, Annie, would you stay here with my Isabel and help aroon the hoose? Ye dinna need t'go tae school the day," she looked down at the older child who was sitting in the armchair by the hearth, a great old horsehair-stuffed piece of furniture which had been in the house when Isabel and Robert first moved in after their marriage.

"Why have I nae to go to school? My Mam never said anythin' aboot that. I like school, Miss Gibbs says I dae the best writing in the hale class!" Annie asked, puzzled.

"Miss Gibbs will nae mind, dinna you worry, now it's time we were awa', I've tae finish fillin the creel. Maggie, will you go intae the closet and bring back ma basket, we'll need it tae pit in the eggs and ither things we get fae the folk in the country," Isabel continued, hoping Annie would not ask about her father until Maggie was safely out of earshot. Maggie nodded vigorously and Isabel set her down on her feet.

Isabel pulled her daughter aside, "You must tell Annie aboot her faither, she is old enough tae understand now, but be careful nae to upset her o'er much," she whispered. The younger Isabel nodded in reply. "Boys, ye had better go back tae the shore and bring the gear hame. I tak it there wis little or nae fish tae be had?"

John and Arthur looked at their mother; in all the upheaval, they had merely left everything in the boat. "Hardly, a few codlings maybe. We'll see tae it," Arthur said and the brothers left the house.

Soon Isabel and Annie were left alone in the house. Annie was more confused than ever. "Isabel, has something happened tae my Dad? The only time folk dinna hae to go to school is when their dads are drowned at sea, Miss Gibbs has said sometimes, or that their brothers or uncles have gone tae Heaven. Please tell me, I'm a big girl," Annie pleaded.

Isabel sat on the arm of the big stuffed chair, "I ken you are, but your sister is too little tae understand, that's why yer grand-aunt has taken her oot on her fish round. But aye, when the boats came back this mornin', your father wisna with them. His crew came back, but he didna, and they say he must hae been washed o'erboard by the stormy sea. I'm sorry, Annie, it's horrible, but he is gone," she explained, squeezing Annie's shoulder.

Annie gaped at her, "So, he's… dead?" she had heard the grown-ups say that fatal word in whispers many a time, but had never known its full meaning before. Isabel nodded.

"But, what dis it mean? What is being dead? I ken in Sunday School we are told that Lazarus was dead in the tomb, but then, he came back to life, Jesus made him come back to life, so why don't ither people come back?" she began excitedly, "If ye go tae Heaven, what is it like? Can Dad see me fae there? What dis it mean, Isabel, tell me!"

Isabel sighed, looking around the room for inspiration. She saw the two large prints hung in wooden frames above the mantelpiece on either side; they depicted angels with vast wings, one standing guard over two children huddled on a cliff, and the other over a tiny sailing boat on a tempestuous sea.

"Annie, do you see the picture o' the angel hovering o'er the boat?" she asked, directing the child's attention to it. "The angels were around the fleet last night in that terrible storm, and when yer father was washed into the sea, that big angel picked him up and took him up tae Heaven, so aye, when we die, the angels tak us up tae be with the Lord, but wicked folk will never be taken there. Your father was a verra good man, so we ken he will be in Heaven. I dinna ken fit it means really, but the Bible tells us we hae new bodies in the hereafter, so I dinna think we can come back. Lazarus didna hae his new body yet, and Jesus spoke life back intae the old een so he could come oot o the tomb. Oh Annie, we just dinna ken until we go ourselves, but never fear, never fear," Isabel felt a tear trickle down her cheek, wondering now if she believed it herself.

Annie's attention was fixed on the picture of the angel. "Can I not ask the angel to tak me to my Dad?" Isabel could see the childlike logic attempting to piece together the situation.

"No, dearie, the angels only tak ye when yer deid, but they will come one day, and ye will see yer Dad again," Isabel replied, gulping back her emotion. Annie turned to face her and big, hot tears began to splash down her cheeks as the realisation dawned.

"I want ma Daddy now!" she wailed. Isabel took the child in her arms and held her tight. What a cruel world was this that took parents away from young bairns? And now the Duthies' newest sibling would never know his or her father. And there was Mary, a new mother without a husband through her own flightiness and stupidity. Where then was the Lord in all of that?

As the day progressed, the word went around Cairnbulg that James Duthie had been lost. Andrew Cardno was at Strachan's shop when Jean Watt, the mother of young Willie, came in with the story.

"Oh it's affa, Willie heard it fae James' cousin Arthur, he wis washed awa' last nicht, trying tae row his crew hame, with nae thocht for himsel'! A mair decent body never walked the earth!" she exclaimed, as shopkeeper Kenneth set out her usual order on the counter.

Andrew felt sick; so it had come to pass after all? But why had he seen the wraith? "And the crew? Did they get hame safe?" he enquired.

"Aye, they did, the boatie wis battered and broken, but George and Billy are hame. I hope young Billy tak's a tumble tae himsel', he's far too often at the Inn these days, and him awa' tae be marriet!" Mrs Watt commented indignantly.

Andrew quickly paid for his tobacco and fled the shop. He headed straight for Betsy's and went in. To his horror, Betsy was crouched on the rug by a roaring fire, clearly in distress. "Betsy! It's the baby! What will I dae?" he gasped.

"Fetch the howdie wife!" Betsy shrieked.

Andrew turned on his heel and ran for "Granny" Penrose, the local midwife. Miss Bathsheba Penrose was a spinster, but her own mother had been the previous midwife, and had passed all her skills on to her daughter, with some input from the Travelling folk. Granny Penrose was respected rather than feared, yet only a few generations before she might have been suspected of witchcraft, such were the howdies' reputation for having healing powers and second sight. She lived at the very top of the village in a house high above the shore, hard by the farm of Flushing Park. The villagers all knew she would be ready and willing to help at a birth any time of day or night. When Andrew burst into her tiny living room, she was washing what looked like napkin cloths in a zinc tub of boiling water. She was a small woman, but possessed of muscle-bound arms and a determined nature. Granny Penrose looked up at her visitor, "Aye, fa is it for?" she asked, wringing a cloth out and putting it on the wooden clothes rack which stood in front of the fire.

"Betsy Duthie, and her man was lost this mornin', I think the bairn is coming afore its time!" he exclaimed, breathless from his sprint.

"That's nae good, she's probably nae due or anither fortnight. I'll be presently!" Granny Penrose replied in a matter-of-fact tone. She got to her feet and dried her hands on a white towel which hung over the back of a wooden chair behind her. From the kitchen table she took her mutch-cap and put it on over her grey curls. Andrew could see she was already shod with leather boots. "Now, ahint ye there is a box, tak' out two or three towels, we'll need them," she instructed. Andrew turned and saw a blanket-box in the corner; he lifted the lid and found the items. Granny's linen and towelling seemed to be in pristine order; Andrew marvelled at this, but guessed all these things were used in the birth process and needed to be spotlessly clean. When he turned back, Granny Penrose had put a long velvet cloak around her shoulders, no wonder folk still thought her mysterious with such a garment.

As if she had read his thoughts, she spoke, "Aye, this is a fine cloak, keeps me dry and warm like nae shawl can! A howdie canna ever tak ill, so said my mither and her mither before her, and it was she fa got this cloak fae a noblewoman that started her birth pains in the middle o' a Highland forest; the deem wis ever grateful as she said the newborn wis the son and heir o' her man's fortune. That wis lang syne, we maun attend Betsy, on ye go!" Andrew stepped quickly out of the door as Granny Penrose followed him.

Betsy saw the door opening; she was now sitting with her back against James' chair, her knees drawn up to her chin, having stripped off her shawl and jerkin, as she felt hot and fevered. "Oh! Miss Penrose! My waters hae broken, the bairn is surely coming!" she gasped as she saw the howdie followed by Andrew. "Now Betsy, you are tae bide calm, I am here," Granny Penrose assured, taking off her cloak and cap. "Andrew, go and fetch her sisters, 't'is better if she is with her kinfolk!" she continued. Andrew set down the towels on the table and dashed out of the door to find Annie and Jane Buchan.

"The kettle is full, that's wise, ma quine, have ye a big basin?" Granny Penrose asked.

"Aye, in the closet, it's an enamel een that I eese for my washin', oh, help me, I'm scared!" Betsy exclaimed. The old woman quickly retrieved the enamel basin from the central closet room and filled it with hot water from the large iron kettle which was suspended above the hearth from the chain attached to the chimney.

"I ken, I ken, Andrew told me aboot yer loss, but the best we can dae is get this bairn intae the world safe," Granny Penrose replied. "Now, set yer knees apart and let me see how far along ye are." Betsy did as she was told. After Granny had inspected, she instructed Betsy to shift her position so she was less cramped, meanwhile, Granny rose up and took one of her towels and laid it just under Betsy's feet. She could see Betsy was shaking. "Have ye any liquorice in the hoose?" Granny asked.

Betsy suddenly laughed at this curious request, "Well, aye, in the closet there are twa or three bottles o sugarallie water wi the sticks still in them! Maggie has sic a sweet tooth, she loves it." 'Sugarallie' was a homemade sweet drink consisting of a raw liquorice stick placed in a bottle of water, then shaken vigorously and left to ferment.

Granny found one of the bottles and presented it to Betsy, "Drink it. My mither aye said it calms the nerves. It's fit the toonsers call a 'country remedy', but it's Nature's bounty, and nae modern doctor wid ken these auld wyes." Betsy drank, thinking that at least it slaked her now raging thirst a little. Granny Penrose knelt beside her, "Are the pains coming?"

"They were... oww! Aye, they are!" Betsy replied, sharply, as a contraction shot through her lower body.

"Good! The bairn wants to come oot, and we'll mak sure he or she does afore lang!" Granny praised.

Annie and Jane came into the room; they were two and six years younger than Betsy, Annie was dark haired like Mary Bremner, their eldest sister; Jane was more like Betsy having light auburn hair hanging loose over her shoulders. Annie was married and lived next door to their father, but Jane remained single, preferring to look after their widowed father. Granny Penrose instructed them to place themselves either side of their sister. Jane took charge of the sugarallie bottle. The pains of contraction sudden came faster, and Betsy began to fear more. Annie put her arm around her shoulder and grasped her hand. "Oh Betsy, never fear, it's jist like every ither time," Annie said, having had two children of her own.

"But it's nae, Annie, this is the last, I'll never hae mair bairns efter this, James is gone and I widna hae another man ever again!" Betsy cried, tears at last springing to her eyes. Jane squeezed Betsy's other hand, "George telt us, I canna believe it, but from fit he wis sayin' James saved their lives!" Betsy's tears came in earnest, knowing that she could never care for any man apart from her beloved James. Why did it have to happen now? Why was this bairn doomed never to know their heroic father?

"Betsy, ma quine, we ken your sorrow, but ye must set yer mind tae this, now help the bairn, push for all yer worth!" Granny Penrose encouraged. The pain engulfed Betsy like a scalding wave, but she strained against it. The agony seemed never-ending as the women comforted and encouraged her in the struggle to bring the baby into the world.

"Ah! There's the head, once again, quine, ye're nearly there!" Granny Penrose exclaimed, her own fingers touching the protruding head from below.

Betsy screamed in frustration as she pushed again, both her sisters expressing further encouragement. Suddenly there was release. Into Granny Penrose's waiting hands slipped a blood-covered baby, but to the old woman's surprise, the creature's right hand was grasped by another. "There is another child! Ye have twins, Betsy!" she gasped, "Push again!"

By now Betsy was beyond caring, the pain, sorrow and loss burning in her heart, but hearing the word "twins", she knew, yes, it was possible, Mary had, and their own mother, Jane Bruce Buchan had been a twin, so she summoned up her last reserve of strength and pushed down through her pelvic muscles once more.

"Good, good, we hae two bonny babies, Annie, take the boy and clean him wi water fae the basin," Granny Penrose told her, giving her the small boy child. She took another clean cloth and wiped the blood and membrane from the face and body of little girl she held in her hands who was screeching like a night owl.

There was little sound from the boy, and Annie could see that his body was turning blue, "Granny Penrose, the boy's nae right, he's sickening," she said. Granny quickly placed the baby girl into her mother's arms, "Betsy, haud yer new daughter close, we maun tak care o' her brother!"

Granny took the boy child and put her finger by his mouth. She could feel no breath. She placed her fingers on his chest, unable to sense the usual rapid pound of a newborn heartbeat. It so often happened with twins that the weaker one did not survive the birth, but Betsy had already suffered one bereavement, Granny Penrose was determined not to let her suffer another. She pushed her finger into his mouth, feeling inside to ensure there was no debris blocking his throat, and finding nothing, she tapped her fingers sharply down onto the boy's chest, knowing sometimes the heart needed a jolt to get it started again. The boy's skin was cold now. She wrapped him up tightly in another towel and placed him on Betsy's chest with his sister. Granny Penrose knew it was up to the will of Heaven now if the child survived. Betsy was tired, she could hardly focus, but aware of the two babies in her arms. She held them close, whispering, "Please Lord, please, leave them with me!"

Granny Penrose, Jane and Annie began to tidy up, knowing they could do no more. Betsy continued to repeat her simple prayer. The baby girl was crying loudly, as if sensing trouble. She stretched out her little hand to her brother's face and touched his cheek, seeing only a kaleidoscope of colours as her newborn eyes began to get used to the new world outside the womb. Betsy felt cold all of a sudden, and looked up, sensing a presence other than the womenfolk. There was something huge, intangible, powerful, filling the room. Her heart raced in terror. "Leave them with me!" she begged, wondering if the presence was a heavenly spirit come to take the boy. She could not see anything, yet knew there was something there. The others seemed oblivious to it.

"Leave my bairns with me, ye've taen James already, leave them, am I tae hae nae peace?" she gasped.

The baby girl stopped crying and began to make quieter cooing noises. Maybe she could see the entity that Betsy felt?

Betsy held a tight grip on the children, and began to recite the Lord's Prayer, thinking it the only way to protect them from this unearthly presence. Closer, closer, the presence was like a cold draught moving across the room until it was right around them. Granny Penrose turned and saw what she could hardly believe, a figure of about six or seven feet tall, in shimmering robes and possessed of enormous feathered wings like eagles was hovering over Betsy and the babies. *'T'is the Angel of Death,'* Granny said to herself. Instinctively she darted across the room, shouting, "Tak an auld wife if ye must, but nae the newborn, leave us be!" Annie and Jane started in amazement, unable to see anything amiss.

The entity turned, a face of burning white beauty, and shook its head at Granny Penrose. It reached out a spectral white hand and touched the head of the boy child, then it was gone. Granny flung her arms around them all, fighting back her own tears. The baby girl was crying again, her little hands both reaching out for her brother who was silent. Betsy closed her eyes and sighed, there was no more to be done.

"Fit ivver is adee?" Annie said, kneeling by her sister.

"The boy has gone," Granny Penrose replied, sniffing back her emotions.

"No, no, surely no? Is one death nae enough for today?" Annie replied angrily.

Betsy opened her eyes again, "He is gone to be with his father; that is comfort enough for me. And he will be named for his father tae, James Andrew Buchan Duthie, write that doon, Jane, ye will need tae go tae the office in the Broch and tell them," she began, meaning the Registrar of Births, Marriages and Deaths in Fraserburgh's Saltoun Square. "And his surviving sister is tae be named for oor mither, Jane Bruce Buchan Duthie," Betsy added, and kissed the head of her new daughter.

Jane, who was in constant demand from the older folk of the village to write letters for them, always had paper and a pencil in her apron pocket. She noted down her sister's request. "I'll need tae speak to George and Billy about James. The Registrar will maybe want a Fiscal's report, ye ken it's happened afore. But nae matter, I've written their names, this date, and the time by the mantel clock."

"Wee Jenny, look close at your brother James and never forget him!" Betsy said to her child, her voice cracking. The baby cried piteously, feeling something had been taken from her. Granny Penrose gathered her thoughts. She washed her hands again in the enamel basin then with Annie and Jane's help, cut the birth cords, and helped Betsy clean herself. The sisters took the babies as Granny helped Betsy across to the box bed. Once she had removed her skirt and blouse and was standing in a clean cotton shift, Betsy climbed in under the blankets. Jane, having found a woollen blanket in the chest of drawers below the window, had wrapped up baby Jenny. She then handed her into her mother's arms. Betsy was now leaning back more comfortably on a pile of pillows. She motioned Annie to bring baby James across to her. Still wrapped in the towel, he could almost have been sleeping if it was not for the now greyish pallor of his skin that indicated the life was extinguished. "Ma darling, Charlie will be so sorry ye never stayed wi us, he wanted ye so much, but he will aye ken he had a brother, dinna worry, dear, dear wee James...your Dad will be looking after ye, I hae nae fear o that, bless ye, dear, dear one," Betsy could not help her tears.

She kissed the baby's forehead, "Now, Maggie's auld Moses basket is in the closet, put him in it and lay him by the fire," she told Annie. "Miss Penrose, would ye tell the Minister tae come? He needs tae ken aboot baith of them."

Granny Penrose nodded her assent, "Aye, and I will speak tae the carpenter as weel. But the best place for him is here just noo."

"Will I get Da?" Jane asked.

"Please, and find Charles and John, they surely must ken about James by now," Betsy agreed. "Charlie is next door wi his Dide and Granny, Annie, will ye tell them fit has happened? I dinna ken how they will cope," she continued, turning to Annie.

"But we canna leave you alane, surely?" her sister replied.

"It's only next door, the quicker ye go, the sooner ye'll be back!" Betsy scolded, and Annie trotted out the door.

Soon mother and baby were on their own in the enclosed space of the box bed. "Jenny, you will never ken your father on this earth, but he wis the best man in this village. He believed in the Lord, and that is fa he is with, as is your brother. One day, I pray oor circle will be joined again, so nae matter how hard yer life becomes ma quinie, think o' the happy end for us a'. I widna say 'dinna marry a fisherman', because that is fa we are, but the world is fast changing, we'll be in a new century by the time ye're a mother yersel, maybe ye will go far awa fae Cairnbulg, but tak care, it is hard, fearful life we fishers hae. I will pray ye never have tae suffer loss like this," the little girl stared up at her, though her gaze wandered around. She had blue eyes and fair eyebrows, aye, she was going to be more like a Buchan than a Duthie. She yelped again; Betsy knew she needed fed. She unbuttoned her shift and lifted Jenny up to her breast, whereupon the baby instinctively sucked her first life-sustaining meal. "Lord, I am grateful ye left Jenny with me, jist mak her healthy and strong, and I will show her the wye o the Bible, nae mair of the auld beliefs, they hae nae substance now," Betsy prayed aloud.

CHAPTER 6

Over the course of the next few days a thorough search of the inshore waters was made for the body of James Duthie, but to no avail. His father, uncle and male cousins had accompanied George and Billy to the Procurator Fiscal's Court to give an account of their skipper's likely death. Fortunately, the local Fiscal, Dr Alexander Watson, was accustomed to fatal accident enquiries involving fishermen. He accepted their statements and gave a verdict of accidental drowning, noting that the body could not be recovered.

Betsy had little comfort from the visit of the local doctor; he immediately suggested that baby James had been stillborn, which was not uncommon in the case of twins. The families, having done their duty and secured the relevant paperwork were then free to proceed with their mourning. The kindly parish minister, Rev. Dr. MacGibbon agreed to combine the baby's funeral with James Duthie Snr's memorial service. The old man had been the incumbent for a whole generation and knew the fisherfolk well; he had a sympathy for them which other landward churchmen did not, but those who knew him were aware of the reverend's grandfather, Michael MacGibbon, who had been the captain of a merchant ship which travelled to France, Spain and even as far as the exotic coast of North Africa. It was no surprise then that he chose Psalm 107 as the main reading at the service in Inverallochy Church which had been built in the 1840s to accommodate both villages.

"They that go down to the sea in ships, that do business in great waters; These see the works of the Lord, and his wonders in the deep. For he commandeth, and raiseth the stormy wind, which lifteth up the waves thereof. They mount up to the heaven, they go down again to the depths: their soul is melted because of trouble. They reel to and fro, and stagger like a drunken man, and are at their wit's end. Then they cry unto the Lord in their trouble, and he bringeth them out of their distresses. He maketh the storm a calm, so that the waves thereof are still. Then are they glad because they be quiet; so he bringeth them unto their desired haven. Today we commit our brother James Duthie and his son, James, to their desired haven, and pray for comfort for the family in their grief…" Rev. Dr MacGibbon's words faded as Betsy looked around the wooden vaulted ceiling of the church. She felt nothing; no fearful supernatural presences, no angels, no ghosts, just emptiness. She prayed silently, "Lord, why? Why take them both? How can I go on without the man that wis my everything? Give me strength, I would fain jump into the grave wi' my bairn and await death, but I hae four ithers that need me. Help me, Lord, I canna dae this alane!" Her father Andrew held baby Jenny who was quietly staring around at the myriad of faces. She had been crying a lot; Betsy believed that the child knew very well her own flesh and blood had died and that she was missing him.

Scanning the church, Betsy saw many of her and James' relatives as well as their neighbours. It was a comfort that the community rallied around at a time of loss, and yes, Betsy knew she could be sure of help from any one of them, even the cantankerous schoolmaster who was seldom inside a house of God if he could help it. Little Charlie stood by his mother's side. He had been so upset by the knowledge that his wished-for brother had not lived, yet seemed determined to be the man of the house today. He was dressed in a smart black jacket and trousers, with a pristine white shirt — the latter a gift from Granny Penrose for the occasion — and wore a black tie. Betsy glimpsed him clenching his fists tightly as Rev. Dr MacGibbon talked of his father's honourable sacrifice, yet his face was devoid of emotion. She wondered if her own James had felt the same when both his brothers had died at sea, only a matter of months apart, and he also the age Charlie was now. The fisherfolk were generally stoical about death as they lived daily with its constant threat, and all shared the risk that a seafaring life presented.

It seemed like only a few moments later the minister stopped his eulogy and beckoned the coffin bearers to come forward. Traditionally members of the deceased's family carried the coffin and took a cord to lower it into the ground; the baby's tiny white-painted wooden coffin was lifted by Betsy's two brothers, Charles and John Buchan, and James' cousins, Arthur and John Lawrence. Charlie and his sister Annie walked forward and stood in front of their relatives then led the procession slowly out of the church. Betsy walked behind the coffin holding Maggie's hand, then followed her father, still carrying the baby, behind him, his other daughters, Jane and Annie; James' parents, his two surviving sisters, Jean and Margaret Duthie; the other Lawrences, including Isabel who was accompanied by her fiancé Billy. Mary Bremner followed with the twins and George. They wended their way up through the village and walked along by the railway line, heading for St. Combs, the third of the coastal villages studded around the area known locally as "The Knuckle" after the deep curve of the land down towards the rest of the Buchan district. St. Combs Kirkyard was where the fishers of both Inverallochy and Cairnbulg were buried as had been the case long before the erection of the third village by Charles Gordon, the laird of Cairness in 1785. The ruins of the old Catholic church marked the site of what some believed to have been the monastic cell of Colm, an Irish monk who had studied with his fellow holy men Ternan and Machar at Whithorn in the Borders before coming north to preach to the Pagans who lived there. Lord Gordon had built a new Parish Church and founded a burial ground near Corsekelly farm which was on his estate; St Combs folk were thus buried in Lonmay Parish, and the others in Rathen.

The old kirkyard was uneven and overgrown in some parts, surrounded by a high stone wall. The mourners' procession entered by the iron gate which had been pulled open by the local gravedigger who was employed by the minister. Charlie marvelled at how small the coffin was as his male relatives placed it on the ground by the open grave. He looked up at the headstone next to them; *Sacred to the memory of Jane Bruce Buchan, beloved wife of Andrew Buchan, mother and grandmother, native of Cairnbulg, died aged 67, 10 December 1880.* Charlie quickly realised this was the grave of his maternal grandmother. He wondered if she was looking down from Heaven now along with his father and new brother. Were they allowed to see? Charlie knew the terrible story of the rich man and the beggar from the Bible; of how the rich man begged Father Abraham to send the beggar with even a drop of water to cool his agony in hell. Rev. MacGibbon emphasised that the beggar could not come to him because of the "great gulf fixed" between Heaven and Hell, but that did not answer the question!

Annie was holding her brother's hand tight, trying to keep back her tears just as he was. They watched as the thick black cords which had been attached to the small handles on the coffin were untied; their cousin John told them to stand either side of the hole and take hold of a cord each. He and his brother Charles held the second two, while John and Arthur Lawrence held the last.

"Will it be heavy?" Annie whispered to John Buchan.

"No, my quine, but you haud my arm if you think it is, I'll help ye. Now bairns, when we give ye the signal, hold tight as ye can till we tell ye tae let go," he replied.

Charlie could hear the minister saying the words of the internment service, but he was hardly listening, instead he dared himself to look down into the dark hole of the grave. The dark soil was black and peaty in appearance. How did you get to Heaven if you were in there? Oh, but Annie had said the angels had already taken their Dad and brother away, so little James wasn't in there then? Only a shell, like the buckie whelk left behind. Were folk like sea-creatures then, that they could leave their "house" behind and go to a new one in Heaven? It seemed to make sense to his child mind.

It was a calm day then, all memory of the storm forgotten. Slow white clouds slipped lazily across the intense blue sky. The sea bubbled and rippled gently below them, the kirkyard facing onto the beach. Charlie stole a look at his mother; the tears were trickling down her cheeks, but she stared away out at the horizon, holding Maggie up in her arms. John signalled to hold the cords tight as he and the others lifted the coffin into position. The crowd began to sing the Twenty-Third Psalm to the tune of Crimond, named after the nearby village where the authoress had lived many centuries ago. The voices were strong, despite the air of sadness.

The tiny coffin was lowered slowly into the grave. Annie and Charlie both watched closely, feeling some of the strain on their arms as the remains of their baby brother disappeared below the earth. Charlie looked down as the coffin settled in the foot of the grave. I will never forget ye, little James, I prayed for ye tae come, but ye went away again too quick. I will name my first son after ye and after our Dad, aw, ye wid have loved him, the best skipper in a' the fleet. A wave of sadness swept over him again and this time he could not stop a sob escaping his lips. Betsy motioned for both of them to join her; Charlie was glad to cling to her skirt and bury his tear stained face in its black folds.

"The Lord is thy Keeper, the Lord is thy shade at thy right hand. The sun shall not strike thee by day nor the moon by night. The Lord shall preserve thee from all evil; He shall preserve thy soul; the Lord shall preserve thy going out and thy coming in, from this time forth and even for evermore, AMEN!" Rev. Dr MacGibbon ended his prayer and the crowd echoed the amen. There was silence for some minutes until people slowly began to leave until only Betsy and her children were left. She turned to take them back to the house and saw Andrew Cardno standing by the gate.

"Andra, thank you for coming, and for a' your help the ither day," Betsy said, sniffing back her tears.

"Betsy, I need tae tell ye something. I wis coming tae tell ye that time, but then... well, I didna want tae upset ye mair, but ye might want tae ken why I never spoke properly tae ye the nicht James was lost," he began.

"Well, I did think there was something wrang even then. Come back tae the hoose with me," she said, realising she had been supressing a strong need to enquire into his behaviour that fateful day. "Charlie, Annie, tak Maggie tae Didey Andra's, your aunties will be there wi baby Jenny. You can bide there or I come back, I winna be too lang!" Betsy turned to the children, adopting as cheerful a tone as she could muster.

Soon they were sitting opposite each other on the benches by the table in the ben of the Shore Street cottage. Andrew began telling the tale of his ghostly vision, "I tell ye, it wis James! He wis leaning on Willie Watt's boat. I thought he had jist decided nae to go oot, but I was as close tae him then as I am tae you the now, and he … he disappeared! He wis jist gone. My heart was sick wi' fear, I knew fit it meant. I ran hame, but then I stopped outside your door. I couldna decide, but I didna want tae fear ye in case I wis jist imaginin' it, but then you opened it! Oh Betsy, should I hae telt ye?" he sighed.

"Aye! Yes, but ye have now. Oh, it maks me feel a mite easier kennin' that you had a sign as weel. Did I nae say then that Charlie and me, we heard James come in? It must hae been him. Ye ken how Godly a man wis my James, I jist think… I think maybe the Lord gave him one mair chance tae see a'thing he cared for. You saw him because he loved the Belger shorie, he wanted tae see it again, and though we never saw him, he saw us! Oh Andra, if ever something lifted ma heart in this dark time it wis fit ye have jist telt me. I couldna even pray for mysel', the pain wis sae hard tae bear, that the Lord would tak' my man and my new bairn on the same day! But no, I see it now, James did a good thing, he saved Billy's and George's souls. Andra, we should be ever thankful that we saw a holy thing, nae something tae fear! It wis James, right enough, but he never meant tae fear ye, he wis saying farewell!" Betsy felt a gradual peace settle on her mind, and sighed. "Andra, go hame tae Alice and yer bairns, ye're a good man, thank you for telling me that, it has given me hope tae go on, and hope for my bairns."

Andrew felt relieved that she was not angry with him. He began to ponder on her interpretation of the wraith; perhaps she was right? Perhaps they were not ghosts or demons, but merely the shadow of the soul who was passing away. "Well, ma dear, I can only wish ye peace for yer loss, but I think maybe we've baith learned something. Folk will haud James in the highest esteem fae this time forward; he winna be forgotten." He rose up from the bench and excused himself. Betsy began to cry, but with tears of relief. She now felt what she had told the men when they had informed her of her husband's death, he was with his Lord indeed, and so was their child.

CHAPTER 7

I love my twin brother, but he can be a great big silly galoot sometimes! It all started in the playground, in our last year at primary school; James and I still stuck together like glue if there was trouble. The wall which had two short enclosing sides was often used by the boys for a football goal, but it was also ideal for the chasing game, "high tig", because we could run up the grassy banks behind it which led onto the playing fields and stand on the wall to evade capture. We were playing with some of our classmates on a bright, breezy spring day. The "catcher" was one of the bigger girls in the class; although she was built like a bus, she was fast because she played hockey. She was running behind me and Mark, another classmate. Mark could be horrible sometimes, but other days he could be nice. My girlfriends and I used to laugh about it and say he must have a fancy for me. I made a leap for the wall instead of running up the bank and was clambering up when Mark clamped his hands on the wall and pulled himself up. In pulling himself up, he knocked me off balance and I found myself falling.

My hands slipped off the cold stone and I landed hard on my back, my head bouncing sharply off the tarmac playground surface.

James was there in a flash. He pulled Mark off the wall and began to fight with him, "You horror! You knocked my sister over! I'm goin' to bash your brains oot!" he growled. Mark protested loudly that it was an accident. The hockey girl, Lisa, was standing over me, "Janey, are you ok?"

"N-no," I whimpered, holding the back of my head as I sat, dizzy, on the ground.

"Did you hurt yourself?" she asked, as others buzzed around like bees to a flower.

I took my hands away from my head and Lisa screeched. "Eurgh! You're bleeding! Come on, let's get a teacher!" I can remember her pulling me by the arm as I clutched my head, convinced my brains were going to fall out. I was in shock, but meanwhile, my brother was having a full-on scrap with the unfortunate Mark.

Ten minutes later, after we'd gone to the senior staffroom and alerted our teacher, Mrs Gibson, I was sitting in the sickroom, and Lisa was holding a pad of gauze tightly over the wound in the back of my head. James had been extricated from his over-enthusiastic attack on Mark, and was reprimanded severely by the assistant head teacher. Mark was bubbling like a baby; he was seated across from us in the sickroom, repeating over and over that it was an accident and he hadn't meant to hurt me. Lisa had sharp words for his carelessness, but I just said, "It's ok, Mark, I know you didn't mean it."

Mrs Gibson entered and sighed as she saw Mark. "Now, now, Mark, you'll be ok, James is sorry he attacked you. Look, have a tissue and blow your nose, you're a big boy and you can't go back to class looking like that!" she said gently, taking a paper tissue from the box on the shelf above the chairs where Mark sat. He sniffled and blew his nose hard.

She turned to us, "Thank you, Lisa, you'll be a grand nurse one day, now off you pop back to your class, Mr McKenzie knows you've been helping, so you're not in trouble."

Lisa nodded, "What about Janey's head, Miss? It's still bleeding."

I clamped my hand over the gauze as she took her hands away. It was a strange feeling, a sort of wet, oozing substance was dribbling down through my hair. Funny, it didn't hurt at all. "Yes, that's alright, we're going across to the hospital to get it fixed. Jane, I've called your Mum, she'll meet us at Casualty, if you can just keep your hand tight on that gauze, we'll go in my car," Mrs Gibson explained. Everything seemed to blur over the next few minutes. I remembered noticing that my teacher's car radio was tuned to Radio 4, as the theme tune from the station's long-running soap opera, *The Archers*, trilled out of the speakers as she turned on the ignition. Mum was there at the hospital, which was just down the road from the school. She was fussing, as usual. The doctor I saw was very funny, he made lots of brilliant jokes about strange things he had seen in the casualty department, and about how his granny would be very impressed with his sewing skills as he eventually stitched the wound which had to be cleaned, being full of playground grit.

The next thing I remember was being taken to Didey and Granny's in Cairnbulg with James and our little sister, Mary. Mum was teaching evening classes in accounts at the time, so we would have been going there anyway. Granny gave me all

sympathy and I got to sit on her lap in her armchair, by the fire.

Mary now had her own little wooden stool, specially made for

her, again, by our great-uncle; she sat on it in front of the dancing

flames, playing with a cat's cradle puzzle. James paced back and

forth in the living room, still clearly worried that he had got it

wrong in the playground.

Didey came into the room with a thin, rectangular box,

"Now James, dinna fash, ye said sorry, the teachers ken you were

lookin' efter yer sister. Come and see fit I have here!" He put

the box on the settee which faced into the room, hiding Granny's

antique Singer sewing machine which sat under the window.

Taking the little wooden coffee table into the centre of the room,

he then removed the lid of the box and put the contents onto the

table. I could see that the lid had a brightly coloured image of

three children with excited looks on their faces; the text on the

top of the image read "*The Amazing Magic Robot*" in golden-yellow

letters. The children in the image were ogling a silvery robot

holding a pointer over a circle of questions. In a few minutes,

Didey had set up the "robot", a Bakelite figure of dark grey holding a black pointer, on a ring which sat in the centre of a paper circle illustrated with questions. A corresponding ring of answers was opposite.

"Now, this belonged tae yer mither and yer uncle. I bought it in Scarborough fan I wis at the herrin' in the 1950s. It wis a' the rage at the time," Didey explained. The game appeared to be in fairly good condition for something that was over thirty years old.

James' eyes lit up; he loved anything to do with robots and science fiction. "Oh wow, how does it work, Didey?"

"Come here, I'll show ye. Ye turn the robot tae the question ye want tae ask, see? We'll ask it 'What is the longest river in the world?'," he replied and turned the robot figure around on its ring until the pointer was level with the question. "Then, ye lift it aff, and pit it doon on the answers circle! Watch this!" I can recall slipping off Granny's knees and coming to stand beside my brother. Little Mary was also attracted by the curious game, although at six years old, she was usually more interested in Sindy dolls. We marvelled as the robot spun around and the pointer rested on the words 'River Nile'.

"But it's the Amazon!" James exclaimed.

"Aye, but remember, James, this game wis made before explorers started arguin' aboot it!" Didey laughed.

"Hey, that's good, how does that work?" I asked.

"Ahm nae gaun tae tell ye that! It'll spoil the magic. Jist hae a shottie o it," Didey replied.

We spent the rest of the afternoon and evening playing with it, fascinated by robot's ability to choose the correct answer every time, although a few times we disputed answers which we thought were now out of date. When we finally stopped to have our supper, I had quite forgotten about my sore head, which had begun to throb after the doctor had finished stitching it.

"Granny, how does the robot know so much?" Mary asked; we had by that time suspected there was some mechanism involving magnets which pulled the figure towards the right answer.

"Oh, magic!" Granny laughed. "But you keep in at school and you'll ken much mair! Ye'll be jist like Dide's uncle Charlie, he wis sae clever he became a headmaster."

Didey Slater often referred to his uncle as an example of wisdom and morality, but I had never found out then how he reached the heights of such success, especially when we knew by then it had been his father, James Duthie, who was the ghost seen down at the shore in Didey's earlier story.

"Tell us aboot Uncle Charlie, Didey, how did he get to be a teacher in the first place?" I asked, "Mam said she wanted to be a teacher once, why did she nae?"

"Well, there wisna the money for yer mither to go to college in those days. But Charlie wis a pupil-teacher first, fan he wis in the senior class, he helped the little bairns wi' their reading and writing. He won a bursary for college, the first boy fae Inverallochy School in mony a year, and he went tae the teaching college o' the Church of Scotland in Aberdeen," Didey began.

"Charles Duthie, please sit down," the headmaster, Mr Fordyce boomed as Charlie entered his office in Inverallochy School – Cairnbulg did not have a school of its own. Charlie, having just had his thirteenth birthday, was excited. He knew he was not in trouble, so hoped that he had been summoned for one thing in particular. "Now, boy, I have observed your work in my class this year, and talked to your former teachers; all of them say you are most likely our best student. I would like to offer you the chance to apply for the Queen's Scholarship; it means special additional study towards an examination in Aberdeen, and if you are successful, you will be able to undertake the teacher training course there. Your study here will also include, after instruction from myself and Miss Grieve as senior teachers, taking the infant classes. This will equip you for your later teaching practice at the Training College in Aberdeen."

Charlie's eyes lit up, this was exactly what he had hoped, "Thank you, sir, yes, I would really like to do this, I want to be a teacher!" he exclaimed.

"Very good, but let me be clear on this, Charles, it is vital for you to attain the scholarship, as I understand your mother would certainly not afford the fees on her present income," Mr Fordyce began.

Since James had been lost, Betsy had found it hard to make ends meet. Even after George had agreed to take on James' boat, which he now crewed with Billy Stephen and Betsy's brother, John, the white fish stocks continued to be poor. Betsy wanted to save for a share of a brand new herring boat which she hoped the men would take on in James' memory, but this seemed impossible. When Charlie heard that scholarships existed to help him achieve his dream of going to college, he worked with a will to reach the top of the class.

"Yes sir, that is right. But I really want to be a teacher. I don't want to go to sea now, since my Dad was lost, I am the man of the house and I will earn more to support my mother and sisters if I teach. My Dad wanted me to be clever, and I will be. I'll do whatever you tell me, Mr Fordyce, but please, yes, give me the chance!" Charlie replied, clasping his hands together in supplication.

"Good. If you are determined, you will succeed, and I am glad to know you want more for yourself than to throw your life away out at sea. You and Joan Alexander are the two preferred students for the scholarship and Miss Grieve and I will do everything we can to prepare you. If you could inform your mother of your intention, I shall be glad to talk to her if she wishes to know more," Mr Fordyce explained. He stood up, leaned over his large dark wooden desk and shook Charlie's hand. "I wish you every success, Charles, teaching is a vocation, and with your intelligence and confidence, you should find yourself much suited to it!"

With that Charlie skipped outside feeling light as a feather. Joan, his classmate, who was better known as 'Joy', stood outside the office, a worried look on her face. When he saw her, Charlie clapped her arms, "Dinna worry, Joy, it's good news! You and me are gaun tae learn tae be teachers!"

"Oh Charlie! Fit news! Baith o' us? So that's fit the dominie wants tae spik aboot?" Joy gasped, her eyes wide with astonishment. She was tall and skinny with long fair hair tied back in braids. Charlie liked her, mainly because she was as good at marbles as he was, and she knew about birds and beasties.

"Aye it is! Now, spik yer best English and tell him ye want tae dae it! We'll get to go tae college ...in Aberdeen! We'll be the cleverest folk in the hale o this corner!" Charlie laughed. Joy grabbed his hands and they danced around in a circle. He ran off just as they heard the door opening.

That afternoon, Charlie did not wait to speak to his friends, or play hopscotch in the playground, or even go and look for lapwings' nests by the railway line, but ran straight home. When he entered, his mother was peeling potatoes, dropping the skins into her big enamel basin, while his baby sister, Jenny, was playing with picture blocks on the rag rug in front of the fire.

"Mam! Mam! I've got good news! Mr Fordyce says he wants me tae go in for the Queen's scholarship so I can go tae Teacher Training College!" Charlie exploded cheerfully. Betsy stopped and looked at him, seeing the look of pure delight on the boy's face. She had not seen such happiness since before her husband died. "Oh Charlie, that's wonderful!" Betsy put down her knife and wiped her hands on her apron, "Come here, my smart wee man!" Charlie rushed into her arms. She could not help herself and pulled her son up and spun him around. "Och, ye're jist aboot too big for this noo. Oh, Charlie, Charlie, yer faither would hae been so proud. He aye said ye were gaun tae be mair than a fisherman. Ye'll be the first in either of oor families tae go t' College."

"And I'll dae it as well, I'll go and be the best teacher ever! And Joy has been telt she can try as weel, so we can help each ither!" Charlie replied.

"Oh that's fine, Joy's mother is a far aff relation o yer Granny Brucie, she will be affa happy tae ken that ye're both getting the chance. Well, noo, awa' next door and tell yer Dide, he'll be pleased tae ken as weel," Betsy said, setting Charlie down on his feet again. Charlie did not require a second telling and dashed out of the house. Betsy looked at little Jenny, "Did ye hear that, wee quinie? You hae a verra clever brother there!" she called to the little red-headed girl. "Charlie's clever, Charlie's clever," she repeated parrot-fashion. Betsy looked up at the old stitched sampler which hung in a black wooden frame above the arm chair in which James habitually sat. The work had been that of her Buchan grandmother, Christian-Louise; stitched when she was only ten years old; it consisted of a floral border and the Bible verse from Proverbs, 'In all thy ways acknowledge Him, and He shall direct thy paths'. Betsy had prayed day and night since the shipwreck, firstly because she knew she had no strength of her own and found it a comfort, but latterly because she felt that despite the double tragedy of that day, she had been given the means to cope. She breathed a silent prayer of thanksgiving for her son's good news.

"Didey Charles, Granny Maggie, I'm gaun tae be a teacher! Mr Fordyce telt me the day, that he wants me tae study for a scholarship and train in the college at Aberdeen!" Charlie had barely come through the door of his paternal grandparents' cottage when he blurted out the news. Charles Duthie Snr was making his way down the stairs from his mending loft, a bobbin of twine in one hand, and his wife Margaret was leaning over a pot on the fire, making jam.

"Fit's that ye're sayin, Charlie?" she called.

Charlie dashed into the ben as his grandfather followed him, "It sounds like oor bairn is goin' tae college, is that richt, Charlie?" Charles beckoned his grandson to come and sit with him in the large armchair in the corner which was draped with a dark brown velvet antimacassar edged in crocheted lace.

Charlie sat on the arm of the chair, "Aye, aye, I'm gaun tae be a teacher, if I win this scholarship, so I hae tae dae a lot o' studying for the next while," he explained.

"Yer father would be affa pleased if he wis still wi' us. Bless ye, Charlie, you'll mak the name o' Duthie kent in the world yet!" Charles enthused.

"Fit a clever bairn, and even wi' that contermashious dominie ye've got. He looks doon on the fisherfolk and their wyes, so good for ye for showin' him up!" Margaret replied. "Now if ye wait a wee minute, I'll gie ye a skim o' the new jam on a sheaf o' loaf," she continued.

"Oh, Granny, I love your jam! Fit kind is it the day?" Charlie asked, licking his lips. He could smell the aroma of fruit emanating from the blackened iron pot which stood atop the stand on the grate.

"Bramble jeelly, brambles gaithered fae the Line," she smiled.

A few moments later, grandfather and grandson were sinking their teeth into fresh chunks of bread covered in the new jam which was still warm and oozed from the bread as they ate.

Just then, Annie and Maggie came in; having just come from school themselves, they had clearly been told of Charlie's good news. The siblings hugged their brother as their grandmother spread more slices of bread with jam for them to try. Maggie, who was now seven years old and in the second class at school had just worked out the import of her brother's news.

"Charlie, dis that mean you'll be teachin' oor class?" she giggled.

"Maybe, I dinna ken, it depends fit Mr Fordyce says. But I probably could!" Charlie replied, beaming. "Ye'd hiv tae behave though, nae playin' the feel jist cos it's me!"

"Ach, they'll jist play up, silly wee bairns!" Annie said disdainfully. At nine years, she felt far more grown-up than both her little sisters.

"We are no'! Dinna be cheeky!" Maggie retorted.

"Now, now, quines, tak' yer breid and jam, and nae mair aboot it. Charlie is a verra smart laddie, and we're a' proud o' him," her grandmother warned her gently.

Charlie and Joy soon realised that their new regime of training took up far more of their lives than had ordinary school up to now. They continued as part of the senior class, which was taught by Mr Fordyce, but they had to attend extra tuition sessions with either the headmaster or Miss Grieve, who took Annie's class. Aside from this, they were given extra books of English grammar, Arithmetic, Mathematics and some novels. Charlie was able to tell Miss Grieve that he had already read some of Stevenson, Hogg and Shakespeare. He and Joy would sometimes sit on the school wall at the interval and read the parts in Macbeth or The Tempest to each other. At other times, they would both head to the manse, as Rev. Dr. MacGibbon had offered to give them some Latin tuition. He had hundreds of books in his library and allowed them free reign. The manse being right in front of the school, meant that the children's mothers always knew they would be in one place or another. The first sitting of the exam was in the following May, so by Easter of 1891, Joy and Charlie felt their heads might burst with the amount of facts they had amassed. They each had already taken a few turns at teaching the infant classes; Charlie, discovering that his sister Maggie had warned her classmates to be as 'good as gold', was very pleased to get a good report from the teacher, Miss Duncan. Annie's class responded very well to Joy's geography quiz; she had drawn a map of Scotland on the blackboard and invited each one to come and locate a place, having drilled them the week previously as to the principal towns and cities of their country.

It was around the anniversary of James Duthie's loss that a stranger appeared in the village; the fisher folk speculated that he hailed from Shetland, his distinctive tongue much broader and more pronounced than their North-East dialect, although he seemed to know their local words. He was tall, broad-shouldered and had very fair blonde hair which was as wild as the waves; coupled with a strong jawline and piercing blue eyes, the young unmarried women declared him a handsome Viking, and puzzled as to why he had come. Gossip had so far established that he was a whaler, not a fisherman. The first Saturday that any of the men spoke to him, they were all down at the shore, with nets and lines stretched all over the shingle, affecting repairs where needed. The tall Shetlander was dressed in a leather jerkin trimmed with grey fur, black moleskin trousers and wore high leather boots with the most fabulous stitched detailing upon them, depicting curious shapes of mythical creatures. He stopped beside George Bremner and John Buchan who were working on barking new nets in preparation for the new herring boat that they hoped to purchase along with Betsy later in the year.

"Aye, dat's a fine new net, is du gaun to the herrin'?" the man said, looking admiringly at their work.

"It is that, and is it Lerwick or Scallowa' you're fae by yer tongue?" George asked with mild interest.

"Ahm fae Scallowa', the auld capital o' the Mainland. Some o' oor men are gaun efter the herrin' noo. We used tae gaun tae the Haaf fishin for the laird, but noo the folk are aal savin' up for their ain boats," the stranger explained.

"I heard that the Haaf wis a richt dangerous fishing," John commented, "That the laird would mak ye go oot whether ye wanted till or no!"

"Aye, but they are aal goin intae fish sellin, far mair money there, like," he said.

"Lord Saltoun used to own the fleet in oor grandfathers' day, but nae now, we fish for oorsels," John added. "So, fit is a Shetlander daen here? I heard some o' the quines telling me you're a whaling man?"

The Shetlander grinned, bearing a set of gleaming white teeth. "Dat's true, I am a seaman, a harpooner. We go tae the Arctic tae hunt da seals and whales. But I was here a lang time back, ahm seekin' a lass, fae here aboots, dat I met at a foy... a dance, in Fraserburgh. We wis verra..." he stopped and laughed a little, "We was close. I hae been awa on mony whalin' ships and I was hopin' dat I wid faa upon news o' her."

"Oh, are ye indeed?" George said, laughing, "Fa wis it ye were awa' wi', div ye mind on her name?"

"Her name was Mary, Mary Lawrence. Her great-aunt kept an ale hoose," the Shetlander explained. George and John stared at him. So, this was Mary's infamous partner in crime? Silence hung in the air as neither one knew what best to say.

"That's my sister-in-law ye speak o', what div ye want wi her?" It was Billy, he had come up behind them without a word.

The Shetlander turned, and seeing Billy was of the same height as he, kept his cool.

"Well, I want tae see her, I have written tae her, but never heard back. I dinna mean harm, I affa liked da lass! Dost du think dat she would spik tae me?" he asked, calmly.

Billy glowered at him. When Isabel heard this, she would be livid. She had confided in Billy that Mary had run off to the Travellers and had her baby, but that she had refused to come home and had gone away with the group on their sojourns around the country. He sighed, well, perhaps the man was not all bad having actually come back to find Mary, but after three years? And Billy knew Isabel had intercepted the whaler's letters every time, to prevent her parents from finding out their daughter's whereabouts. She had been able to pass them on to Mary eventually, as every Spring, the same group of Travellers returned to Lord Saltoun's Wood to set up camp.

"Fit's your name?" he asked finally, after another awkward silence.

"Patrick, Patrick Marwick. I would be affa glad if du could lat me speak to Mary," the whaler said quietly.

"Naebody has seen Mary since you had yer dalliance wi' her! Only my wife kens her whereaboots, so ye'd better come and spik tae her first, and believe me, she will nae stand for ony nonsense, so it had better be a marriage proposal ye hae for the poor quine. Heaven kens fit she thinks aboot you!" Billy retorted, turning to walk back up the shore.

"Oh! Dat is a relief, I feared she had gaun da lang gaet... ah mean, dat she had passed awa!" Patrick sounded cheerful. "Aye, you're lucky she has good freens. Come awa'," Billy beckoned.

When the tall stranger entered Billy and Isabel's own cottage, the one built for them by the local mason who had completed the work just after the first year of their marriage, Isabel leapt from her seat.

"Billy, fa is this?" she gasped, wondering if it was one of the Travellers with some ill news about her sister and niece.

"Ye'll never believe it, this is Patrick Marwick o' Scallowa' in Shetland, it is he who is the father o' our Mary's bairn. He says he's been awa' at the whalin, and now wants tae see her!" Billy explained.

"She had ma… bairn?" Patrick's mouth hung open in shock.

"Aye! Jings, there wis mony a time she cursed the day she met ye, ye left her tae disgrace and the quinie ran aff tae the tinker folks rather than face our mither and the censure o' the kirk! That is a' down tae you! Fit sort o' man, kenin' that he's been wi' a quine, disappears for three hale years and scrieves letters full o' romantic nonsense, but never comes tae see if she's livin' or nae? It's as weel ye saw me first, Mary micht scratch yer een oot still. Ye're maybe too late, maybe she's found a tinker lad that she prefers, that is willin' tae tak on anither man's bairn! Did ye never tell your ain folk fit you did? I am shocked at the nerve o' ye tae come here and expect a'thing to be rosy efter aa this time!" Isabel practically spat out her words.

Patrick looked quite crestfallen. "Did she see ma letters?"

"Well, she got them, whether she burned them or no', I canna tell. So, fit is yer intention, Mr Patrick Marwick? My sister is nae tae be trifled wi'. If you want her, it has tae be as yer wedded wife, and tae gie yer bairn its richt name!" Isabel continued.

Patrick wrung his fingers. "Well, dat was fit I hoped, dat she wid consent, but I didna ken there wis a bairn! She didna write back!" He sounded upset. Then from his jerkin pocket he took a little wooden box and opened it. Isabel and Billy marvelled at its contents, a ring consisting of a gold band and a tiny, icy bright diamond set neatly in the middle.

"Wow! Are ye a pirate as weel? I dinna ken ony man tae ivver hae the siller for treasure like that!" Billy exclaimed, seeing the lights from the fire sparkle as they reflected on the gem.

"Och no, I wis at da Barents Sea for a season, it's a Russian diamond. We actually came intae Archangel efter the trip, and I bought it fae a merchant there. We mak good money at the whalin', but my folk had money, so I kent that I could easy mak a good life for Mary. Ahm sorry du thocht I wis a chancer! I will tak on my Mary and oor bairn," Patrick said, his good humour quickly recovered.

"Well then, maybe ye are tae be trusted efter a'. Sit doon till I think," Isabel ordered, pointing him to one of the wooden chairs by her kitchen table. Billy sat on the rocking chair by the window, eyeing the Shetlander with suspicion. Whaling ship captains and owners might be as rich that they could afford diamonds, but an ordinary sailor? It sounded far too much like a fairy tale.

It was late afternoon, the clouds were obscuring the previously bright spring sky. Charlie Duthie was down at the shore, watching the fishermen work on their tackle. He was sitting on the grassy bank at the edge of the drying green surrounded by the empty washing poles. This spot overlooked the site where his father's boat had come ashore that bitter morning, almost three years ago. He liked to be here and watch, feeling closer to his father somehow. Eventually he would get up and walk the dunes over to St Combs to see his brother's grave. Usually he would tell little James everything he had been doing, but today he just knelt by the small grey granite stone and sighed. In his hands was yet another little model boat he had whittled out of a spare piece of timber. He took his penknife from his pocket and very carefully carved the letters J D on the miniature bow.

"James, if ye had been here, you could hae gone to sea. I think you wid hae liked it, but I canna go, never ever, nae when it took oor Dad. I'm hoping I'll get ma scholarship, and syne I'll be awa' tae Aberdeen, the big city wi' cathedrals and a muckle town hall, and the teaching college! But I winna leave ye, I'll aye come back, even tae the last, I'll mak them tak me back here. Rev. MacGibbon says we will a' be reunited in Heaven, and I believe it, I have t' believe it, cos I want tae see ye, I want tae see my Dad, and my granny Jeannie Brucie. Ye must a' be haen sic a fine time up there, singing wi' the angels. Dad could sing bonnie, like a lintie!" Charlie felt a wave of sadness engulf him again. "Oh why did it hae tae happen? I wish ye were a' here tae see me! I want tae be a good teacher, tae even hae my ain school one day and then be rich enough tae come back and gie a' the men herring boats if they wanted. A'thing's changing, the inshore fishin' will seen be forgotten, and King Herring will rule the sea! But I will never forget this little corner, nor that I am fisher born and bred." He sniffed deeply and placed the little boat on the earth by the flower pot in front of the headstone, before getting to his feet. He patted the top of his maternal grandmother's headstone and left the old kirkyard behind.

Charlie had just reached what was known as the
Hemplins at the top of Inverallochy; it was a series of plots in
which flax had been grown many generations previously. Now
folk left it fallow, as they either bought their vegetables and other
goods from the village shops – Strachan's in Cairnbulg, or
Johnny's here – or grew their own in cold-frames in their meagre
gardens. Sometimes the Hemplins were host to the Gospel Tent
meetings. Charlie knew that before he was born the great
American hymn writer, Ira D. Sankey had come to the villages to
meet the fishermen. He taught them some of the new hymns he
had been collecting in his tours with his great friend, the
preacher, Dwight Moody; these were the tunes now popular with
the Flute Bands at Christmas and New Year when they paraded
the bounds of the three villages as a testament to their
Temperance stance. George Bremner told Charlie that the last
song he heard James singing before he was swept away was
another hymn which now appeared in the later editions of Mr
Sankey's collection, *Will Your Anchor Hold*, by Miss Priscilla
Owens. It was Charlie's favourite, and had been since he heard it
first in the Inverallochy kirk at five years old. He hummed the

famous Kirkpatrick tune which was now becoming firmly associated with the Boys' Brigade which had started a few years previously.

Joy Alexander hailed him as she ran across from Johnny's shop. She was holding a paper bag likely full of confectionery. "Charlie, come and hae some humbugs, I've jist bought a quarter," she called.

"Oh fine, I like humbugs," he replied, and once he reached her, put his hand into the bag and took out a few of the minty white sweets with black liquorice flavoured stripes. "Has Miss Grieve said ony mair aboot the exam? I saw ye spikkin tae her this mornin' outside yer mither's."

"Well, fit she said wis, we could try the paper fae last year, jist tae get an idea fit it wis like. I think that's wise, div you nae?" Joy explained.

"Mm," he mumbled in reply, as he sucked a humbug. "Aye, it wid help. I'm nae sure we'd nott Latin in a country school, but if ye worked in the city ye micht. Folk gaun tae university need it, I hear that a' the classes are taught in Latin at Kings College!"

"Oh ho, I dinna ken, Rev. MacGibbon says they used tae be lang syne, but nae noo, though he did still hae tae learn Latin, Greek and even Hebrew! But then, he wis trainin' for the ministry. Hey, hiv ye thocht aboot this, Charlie, we'll hae tae tak the train intae Aberdeen! Hiv ye ivver been in the city afore?" Joy enthused.

"No, nivver. I hiv seen pictures o' the Kings College and the St Nicholas Kirk in books, though. They must be great muckle buildings! And so auld! Mr Fordyce says that Kings wis built in 1500! Jist think, that's two hunner and forty-six years afore the Battle o' Culloden!" Charlie replied with equal gusto.

"Ha ha! Div ye want tae test me on arithmetic an' aa since ye're sae keen on numbers?" she laughed. Charlie sucked thoughtfully. He and Joy were barely apart from each other these days, he hardly spoke to his male friends, many of whom had now left school and had gone to sea with their fathers. But Joy was family, he had every right to see her as much as he pleased, especially when they were working towards a common goal. He looked at her bright hazel eyes and thought, she's really quite bonnie. Joy blushed, as if she had guessed his secret thought.

"You're better at arithmetic than me! Weel now, fit is six times eight?" Charlie said quickly as they began to walk back towards Cairnbulg.

"Forty-eight. Too easy, gie me division instead!" Joy chimed back.

"Um, sixty divided by twelve!"

"Five! Now, you tell me, fit is a hundred and twenty divided by twenty-four?"

"Joy, that's great muckle numbers! Haud on, let me think... ah, I see, it's the same, five, ye've jist doubled the numbers! Now fa's a clever clogs!"

"Ye see? Ye div ken, ye jist need tae think mair slowly," Joy encouraged. They had reached her parents' cottage; her father, John Alexander, was coming up the lane towards them, carrying a basket of fishing lines.

"Aye, you twa, still swotting?" he said with a smile.

"Joy's makin' me dae muckle sums in my heid!" Charlie lamented.

"Och Charlie, the best sums these days are how mony cran o' herrin' ye hae in yer haul! Ye'll be fine. Yer father aye said ye were a great hand at the readin', aye among books," John commented. Charlie felt the prickle of tears at the back of his eyes again.

Joy could see Charlie's cheeks flush, and realised the import of her father's kindly-meant words, "Da, it wis this time o' year that Charlie's Da wis lost, did ye nae mind?" she said softly.

"Oh me, ahm sorry, Charlie, time flees awa' sae quick! But I had great respect for James Duthie; a Godly man, if ivver there wis," John said again.

"Aye, a'body liked him," Charlie replied quietly. "Joy, I better get hame, it'll seen be supper time," he said, turning to his classmate.

"I'll see ye then, cheerio!" she called, clapping his arm affectionately. Charlie ran up the brae across Main Street to Shore Street and straight indoors to his mother's. Jenny was standing by the door when her brother came in. She tugged at his sleeve, "Charlie, Charlie mak a horsie for me?" she cooed, showing him the small lump of wood in her other hand.

He bent down and took the wood, "Aye, I'll mak ye a horsie, and I'll paint it an' a'. But it'll be a whiley, play wi yer blocks the noo!" he said softly. She gave him a cuddle. "Mak Jamesy a boatie?" she asked. Charlie was surprised that she knew her dead brother's name. "Oh but I did, Jenny, I did, I gave it tae him. I pit his initials on it as weel." The little girl had taken notice of his little woodwork project and knew it was for James. Charlie shivered. Either Jenny was very bright and took notice of everything around her, or somehow she sensed something of her lost twin that they could not.

He realised that his mother was standing above them. Jenny toddled off to retrieve her picture blocks from their tin box by the hearth, unaware her words had caused a stir. "Mam, did ye hear fit she said?" Charlie whispered.

"Aye. It's happened afore now, and nae jist this time o' year either. She said tae me the ither day, fan I wis sewing pink ribbon onto her new bonnet, 'Blue for Jamesy, Pink for Jenny.' She must ken. Your auntie Mary tells me your cousins can tell far the ither een is even if they are at the ither side o' the village. It's something aboot twins. Fan they were born, Jenny kept touching James' face, as though she wanted him tae look at her, but he was already awa'. I think there will aye be a bond there. But Charlie, it's nae something tae be feart o', it's the Lord's gift tae her, and

tae us, that we never forget that James came intae the world,"

Betsy explained in a low voice. "Now, Annie and Maggie will be

in ony meenit, come and help me mash the tatties," she

continued, her tone becoming bright and cheery.

"Tatties, tatties!" Jenny chirped from the floor as she

stacked her blocks one on top of each other.

Charlie took a deep breath. It was a strange world

sometimes. He would have to ask Rev. MacGibbon about it.

The entrance of his other sisters broke his reverie and soon the

older siblings were all taking turns with the masher as Betsy

added milk and butter to make the potatoes creamy.

CHAPTER 8

Isabel Stephen had left her husband with the curious Shetlander and gone to the woods by the castle to see if the Travellers were still there. She knew that they had been in residence for some days, but it was never a guarantee they would stay anywhere long. But to her relief, Isabel came upon the cluster of bow tents, horses and carts. The little girl, Ailsa, who had come for her the night Mary gave birth, came running up to her. She was growing into a young woman now, but still barefoot and wild as a briar.

"It is Miss Isabel, now what ails ye? Yer face is affa dour-like," Ailsa said perceptively.

"Aye, well, I hae news for my sister. I think the faither o' her bairn has turned up in the village," Isabel said.

"Ee, yon's either a richt feel or richt brave gadgie! Fan the bairn is greetin' or sickenin', Mary aye curses the ground he walks on! Ye better tell her," Ailsa grinned wickedly.

"Maybe it's jist as well he's been at sea for this last whiley!" Isabel sighed.

They found Mary skinning a rabbit with the ease of someone born to the Travelling life. She was transformed from the careless, lightsome girl she had been, and was now confident, her skin tanned with outdoor living, and her hair hanging loose about her shoulders. Her daughter, Isabel-Iona, was being entertained by some of Ailsa's siblings, as they played 'peek-a-boo' with a large plaid blanket just at the mouth of Mary's tent.

"Oh Isabel, I'm glad tae see ye as ever, look at the bairn, isn't she jist blooming?" Mary said proudly.

Isabel smiled, yes, her niece was probably healthier than some of the fisher bairns. "Aye. Mary, I hae some news, I dinna ken if ye'll want tae hear, but ony wye, ye maun listen," she began, kneeling beside her sister in front of the fire pit in which glowed orange and red embers.

"Now, dinna tell me, Patrick's come back?" It was the first time Isabel had ever heard her use the man's name.

"Well, aye, how did you ken?"

"Ah," Mary sighed, as she washed the cut rabbit-skin, "Up tae now I've burned every letter o' his ye brocht, but something gart me keep the last een. He had written that he was coming tae find me, as he wanted tae marry me. I jist didna believe it, but then, I canna tell fit else he micht hae said a' this time. So, far is he?"

"At oor hoose. Billy is there with him. He's been asking efter ye, and Billy took him tae the hoose nae lang ago," Isabel replied, unsure of her sister's mood.

"Fit dae ye think o' him?" she asked.

"Well! He's a grand figure o' a man, jist fit I wid imagine a Viking tae be like. I can see why ye taen a tumble tae him. He spiks that funny wye Shetlanders div, but aye, there's naebody here tae compare wi' him. I dinna ken though, he's full o' promises, he's even got a ring! Mary, it's a diamond! Fa on earth is he? He said he wis a harpooner, and that his folk had money, but me and Billy have nivver seen onything like that! It was straight oot o' a story book!" Isabel answered. Mary seemed to be struggling to supress a smile of delight.

"Well, I dinna ken. His name is after the auld Earl Patrick, the wicked Black Patie! He said his mither was a Stewart, maybe even a royal een! I was young and daft, I wid hae believed onything then, but my freens here, they think it could be true. Ye see, there's some o the Traveller folk are descended fae royal Stewart, they were Jacobites that ran in fear o' their lives fae the Redcoats. And ye ken fine that the Lord Pitsligo hid aroon here in a cave and lived like a trampie for years, well, Iona, the howdie-wife, she can mind being telt by her great-grandmother aboot his funeral. It took place nae far fae here at Philorth, and nae one English soldier kent it wis his Lordship. There are mony Stewarts still in Shetland, they ca' them 'Scotties', folk that were fae Scotland itsel', the Shetlanders feel mair at hame wi' the Norse than us. But nae matter, if Patrick wants tae mak' his petition, you tell him tae come here!" Mary sounded excited, as if she was placing some faith in the belief her paramour had noble origins.

"Then fit will ye dae? Mither has given up hope o' ye ivver coming hame. She thinks ye're either deid or awa' wi this folk," Isabel asked.

"I will tak' the advice o' my freens here, and then decide for mysel'. I am eighteen years auld, I hae been a mother for three o' those years, and I feel like I've been roon the world and back again wi my kind Traveller family, so I am mair than a match for a whaler fa has seen the wilds o' the Arctic!" Mary turned and looked triumphantly at her sister.

Isabel returned to the house with Ailsa and the latter's older brother, a sturdily-built young man called Simon, who had jet black hair and dark brown eyes, looking every inch a gypsy. Patrick was overjoyed when Isabel said that Mary would hear him out. She warned him that her sister was very much her own mistress and he should not make her any rash promises. Patrick promised he would behave like a gentleman; with that, Simon and Ailsa accompanied him back to the wood.

By now, Mary had washed her hands, put on the rabbit to roast on a spit across the now roaring fire and wrapped a very fine-looking red and green Paisley patterned shawl around her shoulders, one she had been given by an Irish Traveller at Aikey Fair the previous year. "Now, Isabel-Iona, your Daddy is finally coming hame, did I nae promise it?" she said, taking her daughter in her arms. The little girl had hair like bright copper, almost sparkling in some lights, and her sea-green eyes were the envy o' her Traveller playmates. "He's coming hame fae the sea?" she asked.

"Aye, back fae the big whaling ships. He's been awa' catching seals and whales this mony a day," Mary assured.

She then saw Ailsa running towards them, and further back through the trees in the dying light, two figures, Ailsa's brother Simon, and ... yes it was, the tall, muscular shape of her wicked whaler man. Mary felt the same thrill in her heart as she had the first afternoon she met him at the drapery in Fraserburgh. He had been so charming, asking her advice on the colours of fine silk he was sending home to his sister in Scalloway, betraying a wealthy purse. Then he had asked if she would consent to come with him to a dance at the Dalrymple Hall that night. Mary had boldly accepted the blue-eyed Shetlander and fallen head over heels for him.

As they came into the camp, Patrick caught Mary's gaze. She stood up with Isabel-Iona in her arms and glowered at him, trying hard to keep her affectionate feelings hidden. Ailsa reached Mary first and whispered in passing, "Aye, aye, he deeks a richt rannie hantel!" which in Traveller cant meant she thought

Patrick looked like a nobleman. Mary just smirked at her as she skipped past.

"Here's the gadgie that wants tae spik with ye," Simon introduced.

"Thank you, Simon, jist bide near at hand in case I want yer help," Mary said. Simon followed his sister to their family tent, but stood outside it and watched.

Patrick was now standing about a foot away from Mary and the child. He stared with star-struck eyes at his daughter for several minutes. He looked at Mary. "Du never replied tae ma letters!" was the first thing that he blurted out.

"You didna bother to find oot if I wis deid or livin'! Ye just waltzed oot o' here as licht's the wind and I never saw ye again! Fit possessed ye?" Mary snapped.

"The ships sailed, my lass, I was awa' in Newfoundland and Greenland and even Russia! It was my fadder's fleet, I couldna say no!" Patrick protested.

"Then ye should hae owned up tae yer deed!" Mary retorted.

"But I didna ken that du had gaun doon wi a bairn! Mary, Mary, ma angel, lat me mak it richt noo! Fan your bridder-in-law telt me I wis a fadder, I jist... well, I didna ken fit I felt! Ahm here noo, and I wid ask dee to be ma wife, if I thocht du wid say aye!" Patrick scrabbled in his pocket, and presented her with the little wooden box, then fell to his knees in front of her with a pleading expression on his face.

Mary, shifting her grip on Isabel-Iona, managed to remove the lid. Instantly the firelight lit the bright jewel therein, and she gasped, so it was true, he had bought her a ring! Her heart leapt with delight, but still she said nothing, determined to be sure of her wayward lover. "Fit do ye think o' the pretty stone, my bonnie dilly?" she said softly to her daughter.

"Pretty, pretty, like the spunkies!" the little girl exclaimed. Isabel-Iona's education was purely from Nature and the sparkle of the diamond did indeed seem like the flash of the fireflies that they had often seen in forests and woods at night.

"Mary, I will tak on da peerie bairn, she's mine efter aal!" Patrick pleaded.

Mary finally relented, "Oh get up, ye feel gype! Well then, time ye got acquainted wi yer daughter, this is Isabel-Iona Lawrence, born about three years syne." Patrick scrambled to his feet and she lifted the child into her father's arms.

"Isabel-Iona Lawrence Marwick. We will get her baptised," he said.

"Nae afore we are marriet!" Mary said insistently. Patrick was entranced by the child who grabbed at the grey fur on his jerkin, "Bonnie furry beastie!" she exclaimed.

"Aye, dat is seal-fur, I keep warm wi' it fan I am at sea!" he told her.

"Are ye my Daddy? Mam says ye go on the big ships tae catch whales!" Isabel-Iona asked, innocently.

"Oh aye, aye, I am yer fadder, and I will never leave ye or your midder again!" Patrick promised. He leaned forward and kissed her forehead, whereupon Isabel-Iona wrapped her little arms around him and buried her face in his neck. Patrick held her tight in his powerful arm, then held out the other to Mary. She had stood, watching their interaction, a whirlpool of emotions turning in her head; she was relieved at Patrick's return, yet worried about his honesty, and then even envious of the attention the child was getting, but then she had not exactly made it easy for him. "Tak ma hand, Mary, I canna be the bairn's fadder withoot takin' dee as my wife!"

Mary suddenly felt tears well up inside. For every day she had cursed him, she had vowed never to cry for him, but now the dam would burst after being kept back so long. She began to weep piteously and grabbed Patrick's hand. He pulled her close and she clung to his shoulders, their daughter held safe in the middle, joining up the family circle that had so long been broken.

"Oh ma peerie mootie! Oh, if ye had only written tae me, I wid hae come back afore noo! Oh Mary, angel dat du is, you will be Mrs Marwick this verra day if I can help it!" he soothed as she sobbed.

"Mam, Mam, dinna greet, Daddy's hame!" Isabel-Iona chuckled, at a loss as to her mother's curious reaction. Mary felt the little girl's hand pat her shoulder, and she looked up, cheeks red and swollen with her tears.

"Oh darlin' quinie, aye, he is, he is!" she began to smile, though the pain of the past three years left her shaking with exhaustion.

Patrick had glassy eyes too. "Isabel-Iona, would you go and play wi' yer tinker freends till I spik tae your Mam?" the child nodded readily, completely puzzled at the grown-ups' tears. Patrick set her down on the ground and she ran off in the direction of Simon and Ailsa. He then swept his arms around Mary. "Now, angel, wipe yer tears dry, and put on yer engagement ring!" he said cheerfully.

Mary pulled the ring from the box and slipped it onto her ring finger. The jewel winked in the firelight. "Ye really, really mean it? We will hae a weddin?"

"Of course! I wad tak dee hame tae Scallowa' and gie dee a Shetland weddin, or here wi' da tinker folks, or even wi' da fisherfolk, du must tell me fit du wants!" Patrick assured.

"Well, as much as I love ma Traveller freens, I should go hame and tell my mither and father. I will aye be a fisher quine, Patrick, ye winna change that aboot me. And I want a proper marriage in the Kirk, jist so you dinna get ony ideas aboot running awa' tae the whaling again!" Mary sniffed, wiping her face with her hands. "Ye see, the nicht Isabel-Iona wis born, it wis the same as fan my cousin James wis lost at sea. Then his wife Betsy, fa wis expectin', her twins came early, and een died. Her quinie is the same age as Isabel-Iona. The family wid feel an affa peace tae ken that I hivna been lost or onything. My mither has aye respected the Travelling folk, so she will hae nae qualms aboot me being here wi' them, but it's you, ye see, the word will be roon the village noo, so it's best we go tae them and explain afore the gossips ruin a'thing. It will be at least twa weeks afore we can marry, Rev. MacGibbon has twice tae publish the banns, and I'm sure that he will be kind enough tae hae Isabel-Iona baptised and nae hae the stain o' illegitimacy written intae the register! Nae that I cared fan I thocht I wid be wi the Travelling folk for good, but for my folk tae accept ye, ye need tae acknowledge the bairn. Heaven kens fit your folk will say!" Mary explained.

"And dat is fit we will dae. This verra day!" Patrick told her.

She looked at his gleaming blue eyes and the feeling of love flooded her heart again. She would miss her friends in the camp, but they would be happy for her, after seeing her rage and disappointment at his absence and her renewed happiness at Patrick's return. She would speak to the old woman, Ailsa's grandmother, the matriarch of this clan, who would surely have some insight into their future.

"Come with me, if I'm tae leave my freens here, I need them tae be sure that it's the richt thing. I canna mind if you're superstitious, as a seafarer ye wid be as much as we fishers are, but the Granny, Mrs Elsa Robertson, she has the second sight, and I need tae ken that we'll be happy!" Mary pulled Patrick by the hand to Granny Elsa's bow tent. They ducked inside, and Patrick saw a grand old woman with a round face, strong cheekbones, and a powerful aura sitting cross-legged in the corner. She had a purple silk shawl tied turban-style on her head, festooned with delicate golden chains from which dangled many coins, perhaps sovereigns. Around her shoulders was a black crocheted shawl which was draped over a black linen blouse. Her legs were hidden under a mass of brightly coloured skirts and petticoats.

"Mary Lawrence, come tae spotch yer fortune, aye?" the woman's voice was deep and gravely as if she had lived a thousand lives on earth.

"Aye, Granny Elsa, and this is my husband-to-be, the een that I thocht had left me, but here he is. Tell us fit you can see for our future, please!" Mary replied in a respectful tone.

"Come here, my dears and let me see your hands, fortune lies in the hand as well as the face," the old woman instructed.

She studied their palms carefully, one after another, and then from the little leather trunk beside her she produced an object wrapped in black silk. Unwinding the covering, she dropped a ball of pure, clear crystal into her hand. "Look close at the ball and think on your future wishes, what is tae come I hope tae see and tell you." For what seemed like an age, the three of them stared at the crystal ball, both Mary and Patrick terrified to hope for their dreams. At last, Granny Elsa looked at them, "My dears, the sea will carry ye away from here, away tae a far isle, and there is conflict to overcome, but I see again and again, a rope, a hardy fisherman's rope knit together wi' three strands o' hemp, that is a good omen, it speaks o' a family united. Mair I canna give you, but you maun trust each other through everything!" They smiled at each other. Patrick squeezed Mary's hand; he knew he had no intention of letting her or his daughter go anywhere without him again. Mary felt a sense of ease calm her fluttering heart; she remembered that the three-stranded cord was a Biblical image, maybe Elsa had picked up the thought from her, as the words of Ecclesiastes were painted onto the inner lintel of the Lawrence's home in Cairnbulg, 'a threefold cord is not quickly broken.' Perhaps there was hope of forgiveness now, and Mary would be able to face her family in confidence that she was no longer a disgraced single mother.

"Thank you, Granny Elsa, we have to go, I have tae tell my mither and father that I'm still livin'! I am mair than grateful that this family took me in, and I will mak sure Mr Duthie aye lets you camp here in a' times tae come," Mary declared.

Elsa beamed, "Oh bonnie dilly, you will find that easier than ye might think! God and Nature's blessings on ye both!" With that curious remark, the pair exited the tent and made for Mary's one.

Her few belongings were quickly gathered and put in the large panniers which were fastened to the back of her own pony which she had bought at Aikey's famous horse market. The word quickly got round the camp that Mary was leaving, and soon her friends were all in attendance to wish her well. With Isabel-Iona held in her arms, and Patrick leading the pony by her side, Mary walked from the camp, the Traveller folk following them to the edge of the wood. She turned one last time as they reached the dusty road that ran parallel with the railway just at the Philorth Bridge to see them all waving and heard their shouts of blessing in Scots, Cant and Gaelic. She blew a kiss to them and blessed them in return. The new Marwick family, unofficial in the eyes of the law as yet, but accepted by the Travellers as a successful resolution to Mary's hardships these past three years, made their way along the road towards Cairnbulg and Inverallochy as the clouds scudded by and evening closed in.

CHAPTER 9

When Betsy Duthie saw her son's face she knew he was disappointed. "Aw, Charlie, did ye nae dae well at the practice exam?" she asked comfortingly.

Charlie shook his head. "Failed by two marks," he muttered, dropping his leather schoolbag onto the floor in desultory fashion. "It wis the sums, I jist canna think o them in my heid!"

He wandered across to his mother who hugged him. "Now, now, it wis only a practice, ye hivna lost the chance yet. Did Miss Grieve nae say that it wis a verra hard exam last year? If ye only lost two marks then surely ye'll manage in May? Tell me aboot it," Betsy encouraged.

"Well Joy said she thocht it wis easy, she had high marks! We had tae write an essay in the mornin', dae a spelling test, then general knowledge, then this afternoon there were two papers, maths and arithmetic. I liked writing the essay, Miss Grieve and Mr Fordyce baith said it wis verra good, but I jist couldna dae the division and multiplication in my heid! I managed the geometry and algebra questions fine, but ach, I saw Joy scribbling like the wind, and thocht, it's nae trouble tae her!" Charlie lamented.

Annie came blustering in, "Hey, Charlie, Miss Grieve read oot your essay tae us in class this afternoon! I didna ken you could write as good stories as ye can tell!" she enthused.

Charlie looked up disbelievingly. Betsy patted him on the back, "See? Ye're good at English, that's maist important tae bein' a teacher. Annie, fit wis yer brither's story aboot?"

"Oh well, it wis aboot a sea voyage, a young captain sailing tae meet his bride in a far awa' land and he and his crew were caught up in a storm! It wis exciting! Ye could aboot hear the waves and the wind fan Miss Grieve read it oot! It wis as good as yon Moby Dick, the book aboot the whale!" Annie described, sounding puffed with pride at her brother's achievement. She had sat at her desk in the class, her best friend Irene across from her, and beamed as their teacher told them she had a very fine example of a story from Charles Duthie, of the senior class, who was entered for the Queen's Scholarship. Irene had mouthed "Yer brither?" and Annie had nodded vigorously.

The boys especially enjoyed the yarn with the descriptions of the crashing seas and the ship being tossed like a cork, so much so, that they had clapped with appreciation when the tale was read in full. "If you children can write as well as this when you are in the senior class, then you will have a good future ahead of you. The man, or woman who has mastery of the English language will find doors opening for themselves all over the Empire! The great Sir Walter Scott and the illustrious William Shakespeare still live through their writing today, yet they have been dead for many a generation. Aim for perfection, class, and you will be rewarded," Miss Grieve had extolled, as she adjusted her gold rimmed spectacles on her small snub nose. She was a tiny woman of around four foot ten, but her demeanour was powerful; no student took the risk of acting the fool in this class. Miss Grieve, who came from a farming background, was nevertheless very interested in the sea, mainly concerning the polar explorers and pioneers like Marco Polo and the like. She understood the importance of the sea to her pupils, unlike her superior, who seemed constantly resentful that he was the master of a village school in a fishing settlement.

"Hear that now, Charlie, Miss Grieve was comparing you tae Sir Walter Scott! That's nae mean feat!" Betsy smiled, squeezing his shoulder encouragingly. "Mind fit Joy's father said, the maist important numbers are the amount o' cran baskets in yer haul! Awa roon and see him, maybe he'll hae a better idea how tae stick the numbers in yer heid. He wis oot tae sea this mornin', so he'll likely be back or noo," she added.

"Aw Mam, I dinna want tae see Joy! She'll be blawin' that she bet me!" Charlie moaned.

"Dinna be silly, Joy is your freen, she widna be sae petty. Go on, awa' and see John Alexander, and ye can tak' this fruit loaf tae Joy's mither. I made twa, so there's een spare," Betsy explained, taking one of the loaf-shaped fruit cakes which stood on a wire tray on the table and wrapping it in a cloth. She handed it to Charlie who took it under his arm and ambled out of the house.

The occupants of the Lawrence household were still reeling from the shock of Mary's return. She and Patrick had gone to Isabel's door first, to tell her and Billy of their intentions, and beg for some moral support as they went to their parents. Isabel had decided the best thing was for her and Mary to enter with the child first, followed by Billy and Patrick. Robert and Isabel Lawrence both leapt to their feet when they saw their prodigal daughter. Isabel Snr cried out with delight, thanking the Lord for finally answering her prayer. Robert had just stared dumbfounded.

"Oh Mary, Mary, fa's this wee angel?" her mother cooed, stroking the cheek of her new granddaughter.

"This is your grandchild, her name is Isabel-Iona and she is three years auld. Her father is ahint us along wi' Billy, will ye consent tae meet him?" Mary asked, her voice wavering in fear at their reactions.

Isabel turned to her husband, "Now Robert, the Lord has nae only restored our bairn to us, but brought her family tae, will ye keep them fae under this roof?" she asked, knowing her husband had been furious at the recent rumours flying around upon Patrick's arrival in Cairnbulg.

"Are ye married tae him?" was her father's gruff reply.

"Nae yet, but he has given me a ring. I've only jist found him mysel', he's been awa' at the whalin' since afore Isabel-Iona wis born! But he's promised tae mak everything richt! Please, Da, I bade awa because I wis feart ye'd never want tae see me again!" Mary pleaded, her voice cracking.

The old man sighed. He thought back to the night his nephew had been lost, it being the time of year. *Lord, I'll leave her sins tae Your mercy, I've wanted my bairn back this mony a year past,* he prayed silently. "Bring the man in, he's tae ask my blessing upon yer union," Robert said, after a moment.

Billy entered, Patrick a step behind him. He looked directly at Robert; "Sir, my name is Patrick Marwick, I am a harpooner wi' my fadder's whalin' fleet fae Scallowa' in Shetland. I am the fadder tae Mary's bairn, and noo I ken it, I wish tae mak Mary my wife, and hae the bairn baptised wi' my name, if du wad consent," he spoke quietly and respectfully.

Robert cast his gaze over Patrick's impressive figure and his curious clothing. "Well, if you can promise me ye will mak a proper hame for yer family, then I wid welcome ye as my son-in-law," he said, never letting the guise of stately age drop from his face. He held his hand out to Patrick, who stepped forward and shook it readily.

They had spoken for many hours, Isabel Snr being delighted at the sight of her grandchild and Robert quizzing Patrick as to his parentage and means of living. Mary told her mother how the Travelling folk had taken her in and of the wise midwife, Iona, whose name she'd given to her child. Isabel smiled, yes, she agreed that her own belief that they were kindly folk had been reinforced by her daughter's experience.

By nightfall, Patrick had excused himself and gone back to his digs in Fraserburgh, assuring them that he would be back first thing for them to visit Rev. Dr. MacGibbon. Mary was never so happy to sleep back in her childhood bed with her beloved daughter, assured by the knowledge that her parents had accepted her readily, and that all would be well.

Patrick was as good as his word, returning just after everyone had breakfasted. He was dressed in a fine knitted Fair Isle patterned jersey and his black trousers. Mary hugged him with relief, having woken with the first light of dawn fearing he would disappear again. Robert agreed to accompany him on their visit to the minister to explain the situation. The child was not illegitimate, her baptism had been delayed by her father's enforced absence at sea!

This was the first time Charlie Duthie saw the Shetlander as he crossed their path heading for Joy's house. He waved to his great-uncle, and then stopped as they drew level, "Mary, is that you?" he asked, curiously.

"Little Charlie Duthie, ee, how ye've grown! Aye, it is me, and this is Patrick, soon tae be my husband. He's been awa' at the whalin', so he didna ken I had our bairn!" she explained blithely.

Charlie thought for a moment, "Oh… was she the one born the nicht my father wis lost? Billy telt me, but I wis tae keep it secret," he said in a low voice.

"Ah-ha, and I'm affa sorry, your father wis a kind, honest man. But there is nae need tae keep secrets ony mair, Charlie, Patrick and I will be married and Isabel-Iona will be baptised and nae mair will need be said, so ye can tell yer mither I will be by tae see her," Mary said, clasping tightly Patrick's hand in hers.

"I'll tell her, but I'm awa' tae Joy's the now, I'm swottin for the Queen's scholarship tae go tae the Teaching College in Aberdeen!" he told her.

"Du's tae be a school-maister? Du must be affa clever den!" Patrick commented.

Charlie puzzled at Patrick's foreign-sounding dialect, but nodded slowly.

"I am fae Shetland, dat is why du maybe dinna ken aal ahm sayin'!" Patrick added by way of explanation.

"Oh! Shetland! That's far a' the herrin' boats go noo in the spring, they'll be awa' in the next day or twa. I'll need tae ask ye a' aboot it some ither time!" Charlie said brightly, having listened carefully to the developing conversations of his two grandfathers and the other retired fishermen who habitually congregated at the little sheds by the shore. It was a sort of informal senior parliament from which the youngsters could learn even more about the sea and fishing than they might even from being told by their fathers while helping in the mending lofts. Herring, King Herring, it was the main topic of the moment for the little group of men who looked fondly on the sea remembering simpler days.

Charlie ran to Joy's, and was relieved to discover from her mother that she was out with her girlfriends. He handed over the cake and was directed to John's mending loft when he had enquired of the latter's whereabouts. When Charlie had reached the top of the ladder, he found John braiding a piece of netting. He scrambled into the dark space, lit only by a Tilley lamp hung from a hook on one of the rafters above John's head.

Charlie explained his predicament and fear that he might fail the exam, and reminded John of his comments about numbers. The fisherman smiled, rubbed his jaw thoughtfully and laid aside his braiding. "Well, we nott some numbers tae start. Now, ye must ken, how mony herrin' is in a cran?" he asked.

"Eh, aboot 1,200 fish, according tae the Board o' trade measurement," Charlie replied.

"Aye, right. And there are four baskets tae a cran, and then how mony wid ye hae in each then?" John continued.

"Aw, that's o'er muckle numbers again!" Charlie lamented.

"No, it's nae, think aboot it, twelve hunner is twelve wi' two nothings. Ye divide the twelve by four and add back the nothings!" John explained, "So fit dis that gie ye?"

Charlie looked at him as if inspiration had dawned, "Oh, I see noo! Three... three hundred!"

"Verra good, now the barrel ye nott tae mak a cran is thirty-seven and a half gallons. If ye hae twenty cran, how mony gallons o' fish will ye hae?" John smiled, seeing Charlie had now realised that cutting the numbers down was the way to crack the answer.

Charlie thought about it, thirty-seven times two, sixty, no, seventy-four, and two halves is one, so seventy-five, add the nothing, "Seven hundred and fifty gallons!" he exploded cheerfully.

"The verra dab! Now, fit kinda sums were ye strugglin' wi' in yer test, and we'll see if we can manage tae work them oot," John encouraged.

By the time Annie turned up to chase her brother home for their evening meal, Charlie felt a lot more confident of his ability in mental arithmetic. John also suggested that he get shopkeeper Kenneth Strachan to test him, because, as he said, "Nae man is better at coontin' in his heid than Kenny!" Charlie took his advice and the next morning at dawn, as Kenneth had opened his back door to receive the bakery delivery, Charlie turned up, offering help with stocking the shelves in exchange for some quick arithmetical tuition. Kenneth was pleased to have the young man's help and told him that the quicker they filled the shelves with the newly-baked loaves, buns and buttery rolls — the fishermen's favourite — the more time they would have.

"Now, in the shop I hae tae add up folk's orders and work oot change. I dinna haud wi the new-fangled cash register machines that they hae in the grand shops in the Broch, I hae a wooden cash box under the counter, so everything is daen up here!" Kenneth said, tapping his head with his finger.

"Aye, and you're affa quick!" Charlie observed.

"So, here's the orders for the day in the boxes, I'll read oot the list and the prices. You scrieve them doon and add as we go," Kenneth told him. Charlie took up a brown paper bag and a pencil from the counter and began to scribble down the numbers. He soon found that with all the practice John Alexander had given him the previous day and the little tricks he had taught him made it easy to see connections between the numbers. Just as Kenneth read out the last price on the first order, Charlie was able to tell him the total a few seconds later.

"That's richt! Weel done, ye'll hae nae trouble wi' written numbers, but let's dae the rest, jist tae mak sure," Kenneth said. Some time later they both heard the Inverallochy church clock chime eight; Kenneth declared he would have to open up. "I hae half an hour afore school, jist enough tae go hame and get ma bag, but thanks affa much, Mr Strachan, that's been a help. The exam is in May, so by then I should hae everything aff pat," Charlie said.

"Good! Ye'll dae it, Charlie, ye're a smart loon," Kenneth assured, as he went to pull back the bolts on the shop's front door. As Charlie walked out of the door, Jean Watt entered to collect her order. He caught the sound of her agitated voice, as if she was scandalised by something. He crouched below the window to listen, his curiosity aroused.

"Aye! It's jist nae richt!" Jean's tone was shrill and judgemental, "The quine disappeared and then she comes back, bold as brass wi' a bairn and a man, and her nae marriet!"

"Oh, Jean, now dinna be hard on the quine, her mither thocht she wis deid and awa! I'm sure Isabel is jist relieved tae see her hale and hearty," Kenneth admonished lightly.

"I canna believe that the Reverend is letting them marry in the kirk and then baptising the bairn efter! It wis gotten in fornication, and he should censure her as she deserves!" Jean sounded angry.

Charlie realised she was speaking about Mary Lawrence; how cruel could she be? Surely now Patrick was going to acknowledge his paternity, then that was what the church required? He had hardly ever seen any women disciplined in front of the church by Rev. Dr. MacGibbon, and when he had, their minister often referred to the story of the fallen woman in the Bible that Jesus had effectively pardoned after challenging her accusers to cast the first stone whoever was without sin. Jean Watt surely had a sterner faith than the kindly, patient minister. Mary had come to visit Charlie's mother as she promised, Patrick at her side. Betsy's words were all of comfort, but she warned Patrick that he should realise his responsibility was for life, to which the tall Shetlander agreed readily and said his parents would be saying the same. Charlie decided he could not listen to another word and ran off home to tell his mother.

"Och, Jean Watt thinks o'er much o' hersel'! She wisna sic an angel fan she wis young. Maybe she wisna as foolish as Mary, but my mither often warned us nae to go her wye. She wis often seen at the Inn, a regular customer o' Mrs Carle, so she needna ca' Mary. Do not repeat one word of fit she said. Fan the evangelists were here lang afore you were born they said that the Lord is gracious and wants ilka body to be with Him in Paradise, and it dis nae good for us tae set ourselves up as judges o' ithers. Now, awa' tae school, and I'm glad Kenny Strachan was able to help ye," Betsy told her son.

As Charlie ran out of the door, his schoolbag slung over his shoulder, Betsy sighed, she knew Mary could stand up for herself against busybodies like Jean, but it would hurt her mother. Life would be very difficult for the newlyweds if such judgemental feelings were stirred up against them.

Patrick Marwick came back into the village in the evening. He was making his way to Mary's when he was accosted by an old woman in a black shawl and a bright blue and white gingham skirt. She grabbed his arm, "Ah, ye're the Shetlander that wis here three year syne, and I ken ye're tae marry Mary Lawrence, well, ye micht want tae come and pick yer young brither aff the fleer in my premises, he cam' looking for ye but fell in wi' some locals, he's bleezin' like a bonfire. It's bad for business tae hae men here that canna tak' their drink, so the quicker the better!" Jean Carle said sharply.

"Mistress Carle! I am sorry my bridder has daen ill, I will tak him awa', but did du nae stop him fae drinkin' o'er muckle?" Patrick replied in a surprised tone.

"Huh, 't'is nae my concern, he had the siller tae buy it, so I selt it! And ye should ken that auld gossip Jean Watt has been ca'in' you and yer bride-tae-be a' o'er Belger. I widna bide here if I were you!" Jean commented, with a smirk of glee.

Patrick just looked at her in horror; it seemed that Granny Elsa's prediction was already coming true. "Ne'er mind dat, woman, tak' me tae ma bridder!" he exclaimed.

"Edgar, what is wrang wi dee? Fadder will be ragin' if he kens du has been in da cups!" Patrick remonstrated with the figured slumped on the floor of Carle's Inn.

The young man just groaned. He smelt of sweat and vomit. Patrick was disgusted. He put his arms underneath his brother's shoulders and hauled him to a standing position, then pulled Edgar's arm over his own shoulder and dragged him to the door. Jean Carle stood blocking the exit. "Now, I ken fa you are, ye're a rich man, Mr Marwick, I want compensation for the steer yer brither caused, cos I hae tae clean it up!" she said sourly.

Patrick glowered at her, she was one of life's parasites. He held Edgar by the waist and felt in his trousers' pocket. He produced a little leather pouch and flicked four bright sovereigns onto the bar counter, "I think dat is sufficient, Mistress Carle, my bridder will ne'er darken your door again!" he hissed, as she darted forward and seized her ill-gotten gain.

"Och, Edgar, what am I gaun tae dae with dee? What wye did du come here? Oor name is already in danger o' slander!" he grabbed Edgar's small chin, attempting to get a response from his drunken sibling. He then remembered Mary commenting that her sister's husband had previously been a customer of Mrs Carle, and that she had been surprised that Billy seemed entirely sober now. He may be the answer to this little problem, Patrick thought.

Thanking Heaven that it was now almost dark, Patrick was able to drag his brother to Isabel and Billy's cottage. He rapped on the door with his knuckles and to his relief, it was Billy who opened it. Billy quickly appraised the situation, as Patrick explained he'd just rescued his brother from Mrs Carle's inn.

"Tak him roon the back o' the hoose, I hae a new shed there, there's straw and rough blankets in it, we can let him sleep it aff," Billy instructed. After he and Patrick had carried Edgar to the wooden shed, Billy ran back to the house and reappeared with a bucket of water and a sponge.

"Dat cauld water?" Patrick asked; Billy nodded. Without another word, Patrick took the bucket out of Billy's hands and threw it over his brother.

Edgar gasped and shook himself.

"Gee whizz, that did the trick!" Billy said with a chuckle.

"Dat'll teach ye tae drink! What has du been daein?" Patrick snapped as Edgar wiped the water from his face and sat forward on the sandy floor of the shed.

"Ohh, ma heid! Patrick, da fishermen here can drink like heroes!" Edgar sighed.

"Serves ye richt! I ken the chiels ye've been wi', they dinna care aboot onybody, and they'll hae emptied yer purse tae pour it doon their ain thrapples!" Billy said with a hint of mirth. "Dinna worry, Patrick, I've been doon that road and I came back fae it, but it took a man's life tae mak' me see it's the water o' the De'il himsel!"

"Dost du hear dat, bridder? This man is ane that knows! I canna hae dee meetin' Mary or Isabel-Iona like yon. Bide there and sober up, du maks me sick!" Patrick stormed.

"Ah never meant tae drink sae muckle, no! Fadder telt me tae find dee, he wanted tae ken aboot da lass dat du wis seekin'," Edgar mumbled. He was smaller than Patrick; Billy guessed perhaps as young as sixteen, but with the same fair hair, blue eyes and strong jawline.

"Well, my lass is tae be my wife! Du is nae gaun fae here till du's sober!" Patrick told him. "Du cam' here how?" he persisted.

"Captain David Gray o' Peterheid was in Lerwick. Fadder asked him tae tak me aboard tae come and look for dee. We took da Windward intae port yestreen, and I took a lift wi' a tinker lad on his cart up here. He said he wis camped at da woods o' Philorth. I didna ken far dat wis, I just telt him I wanted da village far Mrs Carle's Inn was. Well, I found da Inn, but ... och, da lads wis sae lichtsome, I bade there. I must hae been there aal nicht an' mornin'! I didna mean it tae happen!" Edgar lamented.

"Ach, ahm ashamed o' dee! Bide there and dinna let me see dee till du's clean and sober again!" Patrick told his brother. He turned to Billy, "I am awa' tae see Mary, if this daft bridder o' mine dis sober up, let me know." With that he strode away, clearly disappointed.

Billy looked at the unfortunate youth. He knew exactly what Edgar was suffering, remembering the first time he had got uproariously drunk with the "Notables", the name used to refer to the habitual partakers of alcohol. The words of James Duthie flashed through his head again, promise me ye will repent!

"I'm Billy, my sister-in-law is the woman that your brither is gaun tae tak for his wife. Tak' this as yer warnin', my lad, ye will never be master o' drink afore it masters you! I'll get ye some soap and a towel. Sponge yer face wi fit is left in the bucket. I'll get some tea made. Isabel is awa' roon at Mary's, so ye're lucky it's jist us," he said kindly.

"Oh Billy, I feel affa, I never took drink at hame, I…" Edgar began.

Billy held up his hand, "Nae need tae tell me, like I say, I've been doon that road. It's nae fine, but we'll get ye cleaned up and ye can tell me mair aboot yer family. I'm keen tae ken fa it is that Mary is tae wed, especially fan your brither gave her a diamond ring!"

Edgar nodded, and began to take off his sodden shirt as Billy returned to the house. Fadder will slay me if he ivver hears aboot this, the young Shetlander thought, and hoped his brother would protect him. Patrick was the heir and their father's favourite after all.

Some hours later, Edgar had come to himself, stripped off his dirty clothes, washed and was now in the ben of Isabel and Billy's cottage, dressed in a large dark blue jumper and moleskin trousers of Billy's. Billy had encouraged him to drink as much tea as he could to help his sore head.

"So, fa are your folk? We hear aboot Shetland fae the men that gaun tae the whaling, and there seems tae me mair comin' and goin' noo the herring fishing is takin' aff, but I dinna ken naething about your islands," Billy commented, taking a deep draught of his own cup.

"Well, there is me, oor sister, Inga, da youngest, and Patrick is da auldest. Oor midder is fae Whalsa' and oor fadder, Robert, is o' the Whiteness Marwicks, but we hae the family hoose in Scallowa'. Fadder is the owner o' four whaling ships, Frigga, Freya, Auðr and Ingibjorg, dat he runs wi' oor uncle

Malcolm under da name Marwick Whaling and Sealing Company. Patrick is master harpooner o' da main ship, Frigga, but he teaches aal da new lads, dat is why he has been awa' here and dere! He begged o' Fadder tae let him aff tae seek his lass, seein dat he wanted tae tak her tae wife. Dat wis a fortnicht ago, and I wis telt tae seek him! I came on da Windward wi' Captain Gray tae Peterheid," Edgar explained.

"Ah, so yer folk are weel aff? Four whaling ships! Gee, they must be worth a fortune!" Billy commented with a grin.

"Aye, maybe! Oor grandfadder wis a merchant, dealt wi' da Norse, da Hollanders, an' da like o yon. Fadder went tae the whaling at sixteen fan it was just takin' aff, and dey got der ain ship in 1850, dat wis da first Frigga, named efter Odin's queen! Oor folk hae been in Shetland for mair dan three hundred years, fan we first came o'er fae Caithness wi' the Earl Sinclair. I think the menfolk were in the court and were granted land tae build farms. We settled in Whiteness and found fishing easier cos there wis nae land worth tilling!" Edgar scoffed.

"So ye are fisher really?" Billy suggested. Edgar nodded. "Well, that's grand. My father-in-law, Robert Lawrence will be happy tae ken ye hae salt in yer blood. His father wis a whaling man an' a'."

"The Marwicks were aye captains and shipowners though, da early eens did well oot o' da Stewart earls, da only folk dat did, as maist Shetlanders hate da name o' Stewart tae this day! Dey took ill wi' Earl Robert for his mean wyes, and Black Patie, his son, Patrick Stewart, was mair interested in haen sprees an' displayin' his wealth tae t'ink o' da islanders. Ah, but a Marwick wis aye in their castles tae broker peace wi' his neebors, so we did weel dat wye!" Edgar tapped his nose knowingly, as if to suggest his forebears had prospered under the despised Stewarts and still remained on good terms with their fellows.

"Ah ha, canny folk then. So are ye gaun tae be a whaler yersel'?" Billy asked, looking at the slender youth who showed much less signs of outdoor living than Patrick.

"Och no, I dinna want tae go tae the Arctic, I wad like to go to da places my grandfadder went, travel aboot and gaun tae college in Paris, France. Du spiks aboot salt in da blood, well, der is little in mine!" Edgar leaned forward and began to whisper, as if afraid his ambition would be scorned.

"Well, I'm nae that keen on the sea these days, but I hae a wife, an' one day we'll hae family tae support, so I'll gaun until I can dae something else. Ye're young wi an aulder brither, surely yer father will let ye please yersel'? I'm the youngest in my family, but I dinna ken anything else tae do, being brought up fisher!" Billy said quietly, having never voiced such feelings to anyone before.

"Well, if my fadder lets me gaun tae College, then I wad read da Law. Der were bishops and lawmen among oor folk lang syne, and I wad be a lawyer!" Edgar beamed.

Billy's eyes widened, "Oh, so ye're a clever een like Charlie Duthie? He's a cousin o' Isabel and Mary's, and he's tryin' for a scholarship tae learn tae be a teacher. He's only thirteen. But ye see, I wis a mate o' his father's; James Duthie wis the man that gave me anither chance, this verra week, three years' syne. I made a promise that I wid stop the drink and be a good husband tae Isabel. I never saw James again, he wis lost at sea, but George and me were saved. Mak' a good life for yersel', min, dinna shilly-shally aboot, especially wi' drink!" he explained, realising that Edgar seemed to be in a similar position to the careless, directionless one he had occupied up to that night in the yole on the Wast Shall.

Edgar sniffed as if attempting to control his emotions. "Du is richt! I maun dae fit is best!"

"Good! Are ye richt enough tae find yer brither?" Edgar nodded, gulping down the last of the tea in his cup. "We'll go roon tae my in-laws avnoo."

CHAPTER 10

Granny Maggie told me the story of Mary and Patrick over several weeks following my accident in the playground. I kept getting headaches and often needed to come home from school; Granny would come through on the bus and look after me as Mum and Dad were both working back then. She brought a box full of old photos and I was privileged to learn many more of the stories from both her and Didey's sides of the family. It was the wedding photo that had attracted me; despite the constant soreness in my left eye, I could not help but pick up the old sepia image of the young woman in a silk dress carrying a huge spray of flowers, her veil of a material Granny said was called tule, tossed back over her hair. Her impressive spouse, who of course turned out to be the dashing harpooner, Patrick Marwick, stood by her side, their arms entwined. He was dressed flamboyantly for a Victorian; a black velvet jacket with splayed lapels, studded with silver buttons graced his well-built shoulders. Below, I could clearly see that his waistcoat was of brocaded silk, way beyond the means of a local fisherman in 1890. Patrick's wedding suit was finished with velvet knickerbockers, white knitted socks and black buckled shoes.

"He was really dishy, no wonder Mary fell in love with him!" I commented, sighing over my handsome ancestor.

"Weel, he caused a richt steer in the village, him and his brither! That suit wis Norwegian, and Mary's dress was bought o'er by her mother-in-law fae Scalloway. She didna want tae be upsetting folk by wearing a white dress, so Mrs Marwick had this een, I think John was telt it wis a fawn colour. But white wedding dresses were jist a new fashion then, because Queen Victoria had een, maist women jist wore a lang gown afore that time, so it didna matter," Granny Maggie explained.

"So how are they related to me and James?" I asked, even then keen on genealogy.

"Well, James Duthie, your Didey's grandfather wis a first cousin o' Mary Lawrence, so their bairns were the first cousins twice removed o' Didey's mither, Annie, his aunties, Maggie and Jane, and of course, Uncle Charlie. After Isabel, the bairn that wis born in Philorth Woods wi' the Tinkers, Mary and Patrick had a son fan they went tae Shetland, but he … he died fan he wis only six months auld, fit we wid ca' a cot-death now. I never kent that there wis another bairn until Mary's sister Isabel's folk came visiting a few years syne, that wis Marwicks an' a', because Isabel's quine, Joy, she marriet Patrick's brither, Edgar, the een that wis found at the Inn!"

"Jings! But how was that, he must have been much older than her?" I puzzled.

"Well, Joy wis a bit o' a rebel, nearly went the same wye as her auntie, but Edgar wis working in England as a lawyer, in fact, it must hae been York, because he found her in Scarborough, fan she had trouble wi' an Englishman. She had been at the guttin', and went awa' wi' this cheil, he wis a ne'er-do-well, and somehow Edgar turned up, he wis in his thirties and her only seventeen, but efter a while she took a liking tae him and they ended up marriet an' a'. So ye're twice related." Granny explained.

"Tell me about the wedding, did Mrs Watt cause any trouble? She was horrible, gossping like that!" I chirped.

"Aye, but she was verra strict wi hersel' and her family. She had been feel in her youth and didna want her bairns daen wrang, but she wis o'er hard on Mary. It wis the mornin' o' the weddin', and it was Maggie Duthie, yer great-great aunt, fa telt me aboot it. Ye see, I bade in St. Combs afore I met John, but my granny bade next door tae Maggie, so I wid often see her. She wis the kindest woman in the hale village, but she never forgot Jean Watt's behaviour that day."

"Oh it's so bonny," Mary gasped as she tried on the fawn silk gown her future mother-in-law had given her as a wedding present. The full-length dress was a very old style, with an Empire-line bodice, embroidered with golden brown threads and beads which made up floral patterns extending over the short puffed sleeves, the cuffs of which were also lined with a coffee-coloured lace, which also appeared around the hem of the skirt. "I mind seeing a paintin' in a book o' Lady Emma Hamilton wearin' a dress like this. Oh, Mrs Marwick, I feel like a queen!"

"And a queen du will be! Dat was my mother's wedding frock; she left it tae me in her will. Du is sae bonny, da frock is made for dee!" Patrick's mother was a tall woman, and though her face was now lined with the vagaries of age, she clearly had been a beauty. Her blue eyes had clearly been inherited by her sons, as they sparkled brightly behind her black-rimmed spectacles. She had silvering brown hair tied back in a bun, which had been hidden under a very modern black straw hat with shiny black feathers adorning it. Her coat had a fur-lined collar, with a jewelled brooch pinned in the lapel. Under the coat, the whaling merchant's wife had a navy blue suited gown and jacket, all of the finest material. Little Isabel-Iona was charmed with the fur collar and stroked it as if it were a living pet while she sat up in the box bed watching her mother get ready.

"Oh Mary, it is a rare gown!" Her mother declared. "And what a kind gift, Mrs Marwick! I'm gled you and yer man could come doon fae Scallowa' efter a'."

"Och, the telegraph has reached Lerwick at least, so it was no' hard for Robert's agent dere tae come wi' it on da mail cart. We just cam o'er wi oor ship, Auðr, da newest een, it landed at Peterheid and we took da train tae Fraserburgh," Mrs Marwick explained, "And du maun ca' me Ingrid, nane o' this haverin' upo' 'Mrs Marwick'," Ingrid smiled.

"As ye like. I'm Isabel, my dother and noo granddother are ca'ed efter me, and my man is Robert as weel!" Isabel Snr replied.

Next door in the ben, Patrick and Edgar's young sister, Inga was sitting in the armchair looking around the room. The menfolk had been banned for the morning and sent over to Billy and Isabel Jnr's. Inga was possessed of a swathe of dark brown hair, unlike her fair-haired brothers. She had her lengthy fringe pinned back in a clasp away from her face, but the rest fell on her shoulders and down her back. She had a little round face and brown eyes, more like her father. Inga was staring at the pictures of the angels as she smoothed bits of fluff off her stiff blue velvet travelling coat. Her nurse had told her many stories of witches, trows and fairies, but never of these huge winged creatures. They looked kindly. Inga felt a little out of sorts, not only with her silly brother Edgar, who had confessed to her his sorry accident, and sworn her to secrecy, but with Patrick; as her oldest brother, he had always been her hero, and now he was to be married and she feared she would never see him at all. Who were these people he was marrying into? They were poor in comparison with the Marwicks, why could Patrick not have chosen a merchant's or landowner's daughter from home? Inga was fourteen then, and the journey from Scalloway had been very long and choppy on the ship, having taken a whole night and half the day to reach the Scottish mainland. She had stared out of the train carriage window at the fertile Buchan fields, having never seen huge collections of crops and livestock before. Shetland was a fishing island; it was their neighbours over in Orkney who had the crofts and farms. Inga had been to Orkney with her father a few times, and had liked the verdant landscape in comparison with the rugged heathlands of her own area. She stood up, feeling her legs stiff, even though she had walked about on the ship for a good while. Inga wandered to the door and looked out at the small cottages, the gables facing her across the street. Coming towards her were two girls, about six and eight years old, both with brown hair a lighter shade than her own. The older one wore a long black skirt and a white high-collared blouse, the younger, a short dress of grey poplin fabric with a lace collar. She had a flower garland on her head.

"Hullo, you must be Patrick's sister, I'm Annie Duthie and this is my sister Maggie, fa is to be flower-girl tae Mary, as she's oor Dad's cousin," the older girl said.

"Aye, a'm Inga. Du better come in, Mary is gettin' dressed in da butt," Inga replied. Annie and Maggie stepped past her and went into the other side of the house. She followed them.

"Oh Mary, 'at's jist affa bonnie!" Annie exclaimed cheerfully. By now Mary had fixed her veil in her hair with the little tiara that Patrick's father had given as a present. She turned to see her young cousins and beamed at them.

"Annie, I wis never sae happy, apart fae fan the bairn wis born. And oh, Maggie, aren't you a bonnie quine in your flooers and silver gown! You'll be the fairest wee bridesmaid in a' o' Belger and Cotton pit thegither!" Mary declared, tears of joy springing to her eyes. She introduced them to Ingrid who agreed with her appreciative assessment of Maggie's outfit.

They could hear the church clock strike the quarter hour. "We maun be gaun tae the kirk, Mary, a blessin' on thee this day," Ingrid said and kissed Mary's cheek. "Come, Inga. Annie, du can show us da road," she added.

Soon only Mary, her mother, the infant Isabel-Iona and Maggie were left in the house. "Da said he would be coming fan it wis time," Mary observed. "Oh Mam, Patrick is a good man, I wis the foolish een, but we're daen the right thing now, Isabel-Iona will be baptised on Sunday and a' will be well," she suddenly exclaimed.

Isabel looked at her daughter, hearing worry in her voice. "Now, Mary, a' I prayed fae the day you ran awa' tae fan you came back wis that ye wid be hale and hearty. Aye, you did dae wrang, but ye hae a good heart, and that's what the Lord looks upon. You and Patrick are daen what is required tae satisfy the law, but he seemed tae hae meant tae marry ye fae the start. It's a pity that ye didna wait, but there's mony a quine been young and feel afore ye, and ye winna be the last. Fan ye come back tae this hoose, ye'll be a wedded wife and a mither, naebody can say ..."

before Isabel finished her sentence, they heard the door swing open and footsteps.

There stood Jean Watt, her face like thunder. Isabel and Mary stared at her. Maggie held on to her cousin's gown and hid her face in its silk folds. Before Isabel could ask Jean her business, she began her tirade.

"Aye, so, this is the ill-gotten bairn?" she snapped, pointing an accusing finger to the three-year old who was sitting blissfully ignorant on the pillows of the box bed, now playing with a wooden rattle. "I canna believe the affront you are aboot tae cause tae this community! Ye run awa' wi' a band o' tinkers, then come back, bold as brass wi' that brat and yer partner in fornication! Noo ye propose tae be marriet in the kirk and hae the bairn baptised withoot ony acknowledgement o' yer sin! Ye should think black-burnin' shame for yersel! We will aye ken that bairn tae be a ..." Mary knew instinctively the vicious word her accuser was about to utter, and did not want anyone, especially her own daughter to hear it.

"Jean Watt, ye auld besom! Dinna you dare spik mair! Fa are you tae come intae my mither's hoose uninvited and judge me? My man is happy tae acknowledge his bairn, and it wis only the fact of him bein' awa' wi the whalin' ships that he didna ken aboot her! So dinna you come like the Pharisees and cast stones at me! I ken aboot you, aye, dinna think folk fae forgotten fit kind o' quine you were in yer youth! Aye, I'm a sinner, I'll say it, but my Lord is merciful, and if He says 'Mary, go and sin no more,' then that is fit I am daen. So, get oot o' here an' dinna darken this door again, dinna come near the kirk, and jist dare ca' me tae ony ither in this village and I'll mak' sure Mrs Carle repeats a few stories aboot you! Awa' ye go, ye evil auld witch and beg forgiveness yersel!" Mary growled, feeling her heart race as the anger boiled inside her.

Jean was so shocked at Mary's retaliation; she turned on her heel and stalked out of the house. Mary took a few deep breaths and grabbed up her daughter from the bed. She held her close, as the child looked puzzled after the angry woman's words. "Fa wis she? She's nae mowse," Isabel-Iona said.

"She's a silly auld carle that kens nae better, dinna you mind her!" her mother replied.

"Mary, Charlie said he heard Mrs Watt saying bad things aboot ye tae Mr Strachan at the shop. She's nae nice at a'!" Maggie commented, wrapping her arms around her cousin's waist protectively.

"Oh Mary, ye were sae brave tae stand up tae her! She's a cruel gossip fa canna bear others being treated mercifully for daen wrang. She got aff wi' plenty, I dinna ken why she's as bitter," Isabel Snr said.

Suddenly, Robert Lawrence poked his head around the door, "Fit wis Jean Watt daen here?" he asked.

"Och, stirrin' the pot! Auld besom! I jist telt her straight though, she winna come near me again!" Mary told her father.

"I'll be haen words wi' her man, she's nae business spoiling your wedding day!" Robert snapped.

"Robert, now dinna add tae it, yer dother's getting marriet, and you're takin' her intae the kirk, let us mind on that!" Isabel sighed, raising her hand. Mary put Isabel-Iona down on her feet and Isabel took her hand. "We'll go aheid, bless ye, my quine!"

Robert took his daughter's hand. Maggie took Mary's bouquet and they began a gentle walk along the road into Inverallochy and across to the church. Once they entered, Mary pulled her veil over her face. Maggie walked up the aisle first and stood in front of Rev. Dr. MacGibbon. She looked up at Patrick and smiled. He looked dashing in his traditional Norwegian outfit of velvet breeches and jacket, white knitted stockings and black shoes with silver buckles. He winked at her but did not dare look round, his fingers crossed for luck. The organist continued playing as the bride and her father reached the altar. Patrick then stole a look at Mary. He saw that she was wearing his grandmother's wedding gown and it appeared stunning on her now slender frame. Der will nae be anither for me, he thought, his heart swelling with love for his soon-to-be wife.

Mary glanced quickly at Patrick, thinking that he was still as handsome as that day in the drapery. Those eyes that reminded her of the summer sky gleamed with emotion, telling her that he truly did love her. 'I love you, Patrick,' she whispered. Patrick beamed.

"So Mary triumphed, and Jean Watt kept oot of everybody's wye for a good bit efter that!" Granny Maggie told me.

"Aw, what a lovely ending to the story! Did they stay in the village long?" I asked.

"No, Maggie said that they were gone by the end of May. Everything had happened as quick; Patrick's folk had come doon two weeks efter the engagement and then his father telt him that if he was willing, he could run the business, the family could bide in a new hoose in Scalloway and Patrick would never need tae gaun back tae the sea. Edgar didna get his wish richt awa' tae go to college though, he had tae serve his apprenticeship on the whalers. Their hoose is still there, Isabel-Iona's descendents still bide in it," Granny explained as we packed the photos back into the box.

"It must have been funny though, you being a Maggie, and Maggie Duthie being one as well!" I laughed.

"Well, I got ca'ed Sandy's Maggie, because my faither and dide were baith Alexanders. Maggie Duthie wis 'Maggie Lawrie Duthie', efter her mither being a Lawrence, fa of course wis Mary and Isabel's paternal aunt. She wis a grand age fan I kent her! Now, you're lookin' affa peaky, ye better lie doon a while. Is your een sair again?" she asked, seeing me rubbing at my left eye.

"Uh-huh, but it's behind ma eye that's sair. I canna see properly if I cover my ither eye!" I complained.

"Hmm, your mither will hae tae tak ye tae the doctor, that's nae richt," she decided.

"Tell me how Uncle Charlie passed his exam, Dide's never got round tae telling us the hale story yet!" At this time, Didey was working at the local engineering works in Fraserburgh, having retrained after leaving the sea in his fifties due to the need for a kidney operation, so we only saw him at weekends.

"Righto, you lie doon on the settee and I'll see if I can mind, there's a photo o' him in the box getting his certificate fae Mr Fordyce the headmaster," she began.

The first journey into Aberdeen had been a blur of exciting images; Charlie and Joy had arrived at the railway station in Guild Street accompanied by their headmaster, and were immediately dazzled by the architectural grandeur of Her Majesty's Theatre and Opera House situated just across from the station. Each of the windows and doors were surmounted by an arch of multi-coloured bricks, giving the appearance of some exotic foreign venue. Ladies with fine day-dresses and parasols paraded along the pavement in front of it, and Joy cooed over their expensive attire. Mr Fordyce had directed them up Market Street, not before Charlie glanced at the harbour full of high-masted Fifies and Zulus, and the new steam-powered fishing boats that he had heard so much about from his relatives.

They climbed aboard a horse-tram at St. Nicholas Street outside a hotel with the entrance on a pretty curved corner. Mr Fordyce explained that opposite them had been a marble statue of Queen Victoria, but this had been moved into the Town's House three years previously. The tram pulled smoothly along the tracks as the sturdy Clydesdale horse clip-clopped up onto George Street. There were so many large shops selling everything under the sun, including drapers, china merchants, booksellers, cutlers, tobacconists and grocers. Eventually they heard the tram conductor shout *"Training College!"* which was the signal to alight. The Church of Scotland Teacher Training

College was an impressive building indeed; the religious influence was clear in the pointed gables on the roof, but there was something positively medieval about the stately bell tower with its conical roof.

Very soon Charlie and Joy were ushered into a large room full of desks where other children their age were already seating themselves. Once the desks were full, they were addressed by a man in a black academic robe who introduced himself as Mr Ogilvie, the Rector of the college. He explained the rules for the four papers that they would sit that day and wished them well in their endeavours. Charlie would recall long after the horror of turning over the paper and seeing the words Arithmetic, his bête-noire was first! Yet all the practice and tricks that he had been taught by Joy's father and Kenneth Strachan came back to him; he actually enjoyed totting up the numbers and working out the longer sums involving division and multiplication. The other papers were taxing, but less so than the previous year's exam they had tried over a month ago now.

It was now a fortnight later, and Charlie was returning with Miss Grieve to the college to collect his certificate and his scholarship. Mr Fordyce had not been able to come, but had praised his achievement in front of the whole school. It was a bitter-sweet victory as poor Joy had failed by one mark, in her English interpretation paper. She hid her disappointment well, joking with Charlie that she had spent too much time on her numerical study, but he knew she was upset. There was another chance next year though, she would manage then, she told him. Charlie was wearing a new blazer, bought from the Corner Drapery in Fraserburgh the day he received the news of his success, black school trousers, white shirt and even a tie. Miss Grieve had been telling him that although the college only provided boarding for female students, his scholarship would allow for accommodation in the city should he wish it.

George Street was so loud and bustling, Charlie could not imagine being able to sleep at night amongst such clamour. Back in the large college hall again, Charlie was joined by the other successful scholars. The Rector, Mr Ogilvie and another man also in robes — whom Miss Grieve mentioned was Professor Milligan, the chairman of the Church of Scotland's Education Committee for Aberdeen — stood at the back of the room where many large honours boards displayed the names of graduates and prize winners dating back over the last few decades.

"Charles Duthie, Inverallochy School, Fraserburgh," Mr Ogilvie called out. Charles felt his heart leap as he stood up and walked up to the grand academics. Mr Ogilvie shook his hand, "Well done, Charles, you are the only candidate from your school this year to have gained a Queen's Scholarship, Professor Milligan will present you with your certificate of achievement," he said loudly. The professor had a white beard, reminding Charlie of the oldest fisherman in the village, Jocky Slater, who was still taking his yole to sea at the age of eighty.

"Mr Duthie, congratulations," he boomed, and handed him a scroll of paper tied with a red ribbon. "And indeed, we have another award for you, your composition piece not only gained the highest marks in the whole year, but was so popular with the examiners, that you will also receive the Burnett-Guild Essay Prize for 1891. This prize was instituted by two members of the Hammermen's Guild of the Seven Incorporated Trades, one of whom, Mr William Guild, is a descendant of Rev. Dr. Guild, the first patron of that organisation and former principal of Kings College. Both he and his colleague believed that the ability to communicate well by the written word was vital to academic progress, and thus they funded this award to recognise such talent. The examiners were particularly impressed by your realistic descriptions of the sea voyage, which they say, and I agree, having read it myself, show you may even have promise as a great author. I think you will certainly therefore make a fine teacher, and we will be glad to welcome you at the start of the autumn term," Professor Milligan explained.

A spontaneous round of applause rippled through the room, started, Charlie suspected by Miss Grieve. He blushed; he had merely re-written the story he had entered in the practice exam, but spent more time talking about the captain steering through the storm than the romantic section at the end where he reached his bride safely. He had been thinking of his father as he wrote of the waves and the whistle of the wind, feeling entirely at home in his imagination.

The essay prize was a little silver medal and another certificate. Charlie was then shown around the college with the other children who would be his fellow students in September.

The room in which the exam had taken place was the main lecture room, there were smaller classrooms attached and then outside, across the yard on the Charlotte Street side, they were shown into the Practising School. "This is where you will either take classes as some of you have already done in your own schools, or watch the teaching staff hold model lessons. The government and the church inspectors visit us every few years to ensure our methods are of the highest standard. Come, if we step up into the viewing area here, you will be able to watch the class in progress with their student teacher. They will not be disturbed as the window here is mirrored," Mr Ogilvie explained quietly as the little group of twenty children, between thirteen and fourteen, followed him.

The following year, Charlie was the student standing in front of the class, well aware that the trotting of feet by his door meant that the scholarship winners were being shown around the college. Joy Alexander was able to pass her exam and it was that term that Charlie had made arrangements to move to the city. Joy's parents were quite relieved to know he would be there to keep an eye on her in this new situation. It was hard for them to see each other during the day because they were in different classes, but in the evening, they would meet up and go to Mrs Adams' little restaurant near Beattie's Court or to the entertainments at the Northern Friendly Society's Hall at the corner of St Andrew Street. On a Saturday, many of the students would head to the theatre on Guild Street for the afternoon matinee performances. Usually there would be a variety show with singing, dancing and magician acts; the male students could visit the Criterion Bar next door to the theatre at interval time, as there was a convenient bell in the bar which rang when the next act was due to start. Charlie hardly ever went to the bar, maintaining his teetotal stance. One particular afternoon he was standing in the foyer, having bought a box of sugared almonds at the booth to share later with Joy, when a young man with very fair blonde hair and blue eyes stood before him and greeted him.

"Charlie Duthie?" Charlie nodded, "Dost du nae ken me?" the voice was instantly recognisable.

"Edgar Marwick! I thought ye'd gone back tae Shetland tae the whaling ships!" he exclaimed.

"Aye, I did, but I've finally persuaded ma fadder tae let me gaun tae college and study law. But, Patrick has arranged for me tae work at a solicitor's office here first, mak' sure I can dae the work! Ahm tae be a clerk until I can gaun tae Kings College in October, better I ken the law o' Scotland before I gaun tae France!" he explained. He was dressed very finely in a pale blue velvet short jacket with embroidered lapels and cuffs, a navy blue cravat around his neck, tucked into a collarless shirt, black trousers, and he carried a top hat trimmed with a ribbon the same colour as his jacket. He looked for all the world like a dandy from the Georgian era.

"Well, that's grand! And how is Mary and the bairn?" Charlie asked.

"Thrivin', baith o them. Mary is gaun wi' anither baby, and oor fadder is hoping it is a laddie, a "proper heir" he says! Mary didna look weel on dat!" Edgar replied. "Better ahm nae there!"

Just then the bell rang for the end of the interval; Joy and her good friend Rosemary Chandler appeared from the ladies' waiting room. "Come awa', Charlie," Joy began, "Oh, fa's this fine chiel?" she smiled, nudging her friend.

"Div ye nae mind on Edgar? Patrick's brither? Een o' the Shetlanders, he's here tae be a solicitor's clerk!" Charlie explained. "Ah, that's richt, you were at yer brither's wedding! Rosemary, this man's father owns four whaling ships and has his ain company!" Joy told her.

"Er, aye, ahm da youngest laddie, ah've been a sailor in the Arctic da last twa year, my fadder gives me an allowance an' dat is aal I hae, so da quicker I get started ma new job, da better!" Edgar chuckled with a wave of his hat, "But pleased tae meet ye, ladies, are ye liking da spree?"

Joy and Rosemary tittered, Edgar's Shetland dialect being a little beyond them.

"He means the show! Shetlanders dinna speak like us!" Charlie laughed.

"I've never met anybody from Shetland before, I thought you were all Vikings!" Rosemary exclaimed cheerfully, "You see, I was born in the city, in Kittybrewster, it's all farmers and railwaymen beside us!" she added.

"Ah well, we hae nae fairmers or railways in Shetland! There is jist enough land for the barest o' croftin', but it's Orkney ye get fairmers!" Edgar replied.

"You'll have to come tae the mart then, on auction day, you'll see coos, sheep, pigs, everything!" Rosemary said.

"Oh well, if dat's an invitation, I'll be happy tae come! But I must get back tae my lads, dey are aal in the office I'll be workin' in, so I'm jist gettin' tae ken them," he told them all. He bowed with an extravagant flourish, and turned to go, "Charlie, my lodgings are in Schoolhill, with a Mrs Mitchell, number 68, call by sometime!" Edgar called over his shoulder.

"Ooh, what a gentleman!" Rosemary giggled as they returned to their seats.

"Och now, dinna be taken in, Edgar's nae perfect," Charlie commented; he remembered the gossip, Edgar had spent everything he had at the Inn when he first arrived and Patrick had to remove him after he was dead drunk.

"Havers! He's a fine figure o' a man. He canna be that hallirackit if he's tae be a solicitor's clerk!" Joy chimed in, "Dinna mind him, Rosemary, the auld mither hen!"

Charlie was a little crestfallen; he did not like the idea of the flamboyant Shetlander coming to woo Rosemary, he had quite liked the idea of courting her himself. Joy and Rosemary sat either side of Charlie when they returned to the auditorium. Joy whispered in his ear, "Dinna tell me ye're jealous o' Edgar?" Charlie did not look round, but mouthed "No, I'm nae, fit wye should I be?"

Joy just laughed, she could see a red tinge around her friend's ears, oh yes, she had noticed that he paid attention to Rosemary, always listened to her, deferred to her in conversation, but stopped short of spending all his free time with her. Perhaps it had only occurred to him at that moment that he was taking a fancy to her friend? Rosemary was so different; she spoke English more often than Scots, her father owned a grocer's shop in Clifton Road, and she had visited lots of places where there were markets and wholesalers from whom her father bought his stock. She loved the Belmont Mart and took great delight in adding facts about livestock to her demonstration lessons. Joy and she had travelled out to Clinterty in her father's phaeton carriage to the Chandler's family farm, still owned by Rosemary's grandfather, but managed by her uncle. Joy puzzled as to whether Charlie would go with a girl who had no connections to the fisher way of life, yet Rosemary seemed quite flattered by the attentions of the young whaler.

"Plenty time, Charlie, we've got to get through all our training yet!" was Joy's assured reply.

He found it hard to concentrate on the antics of the ventriloquist which began the second act. The young male performer was making a sterling job of throwing his voice so it appeared to emanate from the mouth of the wooden doll dressed in an outlandish red suit which 'sat' on the performer's lap.

Charlie stole a look at Rosemary; she was tall and slender, having curly brown hair which she had pinned back from her face in a French Roll style. He liked how the curls formed a little halo around her face, and that her nose wrinkled when she smiled. She was very freckled, but he realised how attractive that was with her large brown eyes. Freckled folk had been teased mercilessly at school, how silly, he thought, she's pretty indeed. She caught his gaze for a moment and grinned as if she knew what he was thinking. Charlie forced himself to look back at the stage, where the performer was causing his doll to do a little dance while singing a nonsense song. Joy and Rosemary then exchanged glances and giggled. Charlie felt rather uncomfortable now, what had he started?

CHAPTER 11

It was hard to believe that falling off a wall would mean that I would have to wear spectacles. I was horrified; no, not glasses! I would be a laughing stock. It was a whole year since the playground incident, but finally Mum had paid attention to my Granny's pleas to attend to my headaches and sore eyes. It was a bit of a mess really, she felt guilty for not noticing, Dad got mad that she was spending too many days at work when she did not need to do full-time and James, as usual, had vowed he would batter anybody who was rude to me about it. The upshot was that I had an operation; at eleven years old, my eyes had already developed, so any damage now was very likely to be permanent, but the doctor, the ophthalmic surgeon, let's get it right, said he was willing to try to repair whatever was wrong in there.

It was quite fun in hospital really; Sick Children's Aberdeen was still an old Victorian building then, full of high-ceilinged wards, nurses in blue and pink dresses, and a fearful dragon of a ward sister that they ran in terror of. Thinking back now, I was only there for two and a half days, but it seemed ages.

Amazingly Mark Cameron, the same boy who had banged into

me on the wall was in at the same time. He was getting his

tonsils out. He was pretty gloomy as his throat was so sore and

itchy before his operation. I really got to like him then, even

though he could hardly speak, we played Hangman on all the

spare bits of paper we could find. We wound up the nurses the

first night by daring all the children on our side of the ward to ask

permission to go to the toilet. After four of us went, they were

getting wise to our little game, and we were chased back to bed

with threats of "I'll get the Matron to you silly bairns! Get to

bed!"

I was due to get my operation around 11 o'clock the next

day, so was delighted when my brother turned up with our Uncle

Sandy, Alexander Slater, Mum's only brother. Sandy was a

fisherman, the skipper on one of the brand new pelagic trawlers

out of Peterhead and he was very successful time, as were many

skippers in the North East. Peterhead was boom-town, which

was really exciting, as Aberdeen had always been held up to us as the city, but now our fishermen were outfishing and outselling any of the North of England trawlers.

"I got a half-day! Mum and Dad gave me a note so I could come in and see you! Mary's at home with Auntie Laura, and we've got a story to tell you!" James enthused, jumping onto the bed.

Now, now, ma loon, sit on the chair, yer sister's awa' tae hae a serious operation!" Sandy scolded lightly.

"What? What is it?" I asked.

"Know how Mum's been really sick and gloomy lately? Well, she said she had been to the doctor, and ... we're going to hae a new brother or sister!" James exploded.

"Really?" I was incredulous, our sister was seven years old, surely Mum couldn't be having more children now? But what did we know then?

"Yes, aye, yer mither is expectin', so I think yer father's pleased she'll bide at hame at last! My sister Betsy works far too hard, she aye has! Onywye, yer auntie Laura and me will look efter you eens for a while till yer folks get themselves organised," Sandy explained.

"Oh great! That'll be fun. Auntie Laura makes the best cakes in the world!" I enthused, imagining the cakestands full of goodies that my mother's sister-in-law always provided when we went to visit. "I hope she's going to make a Victoria Sponge for me when I get out o' here, the doctor said I've got to wear an eye-patch! I dinna want to go back to school till I can see properly again!"

"Ah, ye'll be fine! I'll pit in your order the nicht then. Doctors are affa advanced nowadays, has your Didey ever telt you the story of how he lost his pinkie?" Sandy began. He was almost as good a storyteller as his father, having that same couthy way about him, suffused with the wisdom of the generations past.

James and I looked at eachother, yes, we all knew about Didey John's missing pinkie finger, but he would never tell the truth about it. We had heard every excuse in the book from '*Oh, I didna suck my thumb fan I wis a boy, it wis my pinkie, and een nicht I sucked it clean aff!*' to "*Well, it really happened fan twa boats gid agither in the harbour!*" "No, but he's made up plenty stories about it!" James laughed.

"Well, it wis afore ony o' us were born, even afore oor folks got marriet. Aye, they were engaged, but the Second World War got in the wye! Now my faither was only nineteen fan the war broke oot, but as a fisherman he joined the Royal Naval Reserve, fit they ca'ed the 'Wavy Navy', cos the skippers fa got commissions hid wavy stripes on their uniforms.

Oor Didey, fa I'm ca'ed efter, Sandy Slater, he wis too auld at sixty-four tae be called up, so he wis able tae bide at hame and be in the Civil Defence, something Granny Annie wis affa happy aboot… onywye, mony boats fae roon this corner were commandeered by the Navy, so the skippers jist took them far they were needed, and one place wis the Orkney Isles. Even in the First War, the British Grand fleet lay at anchor there, and I wis telt by my faither's crewmate, his cousin, Sandy Wood, that it happened the nicht the *Royal Oak* wis sunk in Scapa Flow by a German torpedo. Their boat wis anchored tae the *Pegasus*, which wis an auld sea plane, jist nae far fae *Royal Oak*, and fan the explosions came in the middle o' the nicht, a'body wis trying tae move at once tae gaun tae the aid o' the sailors…

"Haul up the hawser!" John and Sandy heard their skipper, fellow Belger, Robert Mair yell. They had been asleep in their bunks when a huge bang followed by a shattering, crunching sound exploded into the still night across Scapa Flow. The two cousins leapt up and hurriedly pulled on their seaboots.

"Fit's happened, Skipper?" John asked, as he passed the wheelhouse window, out of which Robert was leaning.

"The *Royal Oak's* on fire. Something's blown her up! Folk are sayin' it wis a U-Boat, but that canna be possible! G'wa and help pull up the anchor, we need tae help! The *Daisy II* wis tied tae her, so they'll be first on site," Robert explained quickly.

The crew moved as quickly as they could to get the boat ready; Robert barked instructions to the fireman in the engine room via the speaking tube in the wheelhouse. Very soon the Brazen Serpent's funnel was pumping out steam and the trawler was underway. John had just finished checking the ropes were all aboard when he saw another boat, a local Orcadian trawler come alongside.

The swell as the two vessels passed each other caused John to fall forward; he grabbed onto the rail to stop himself falling overboard and felt the side of the other trawler squash against his hand, he howled and pulled his hand free. Although all vessels in the area had their lights either covered or out, the Northern Lights had been making the sky as bright as noonday as they flickered and danced across the October night. Sandy heard John's cry and came over to him, "Fit happened? Are ye a'right?" he asked.

"Och aye, jist dunted my hand there, oor neeper boat jist pushed past," John replied.

"See yer hand," Sandy said. John lifted up his right hand and his cousin grabbed his wrist in horror, "Johnny, gee whizz min, yer cranny's in bits! Skipper! Skipper, we've got a casualty!"

"Eh?" John stared at his hand, yes he'd felt the impact and guessed his fingers would be bruised, but he was not prepared for the sight of his little finger. The skin had been sheared off the top above the knuckle, the top part of the finger bone had gone, a broken stump remaining, and blood poured down his hand. He instantly felt sick. "Oh no," he muttered. Sandy hauled him across to the wheelhouse where Robert gaped at his crewman's injury.

"Oh John, fit are we tae dae with ye? Sandy, get that tied up afore he bleeds tae death!" the skipper ordered. Sandy sat John down on the bench seat behind the wheel. He looked about him and spotted the tin first aid box. From inside he extracted a crepe bandage and wrapped it tightly around John's hand, immobilising the damaged finger.

"That should dae until we can get help," Sandy said.

"Well, it's nae bad, I dinna feel it," John said, although his stomach was still queasy.

"Good, get up here and help ma keep an eye on things, I can see the *Daisy II*, I'll try radioing him," Robert commented. The ship to ship radio was a real boon during the conflict; Robert had been delighted when the Navy had paid for a radio to be installed in the Brazen Serpent. There was loud static crackle and suddenly they heard the familiar voice of John Gatt, skipper of *Daisy II*, a thirty-year old steel trawler built in Torry for the Mays of Cairnbulg, well-known to the crew.

"It's like Hades itsel' in here, Rob, far are ye?" John yelled.

"On oor wye, John, we've an Orcadian aside us, we'll be wi' ye in meenits," Robert replied. "Fit happened? Wis it a sub?"

"Aye it wis! We felt the whoosh o' the torpedoes! Aw, Rob, there wis a gang o' young lads onboard, they're a' deid according tae the captain, the explosion blew up their magazine an' a'. We can hardly see, but for the Aurora Borealis, so pit yer lichts on fan ye come by, I dinna think Jerry's coming back the now!" he bawled, as the noise of shouting voices and screams filled the background of his transmission.

"Haud on, John, comin' as fast as we can, over," Robert told him, his heart sinking. If this was the sign of things to come it would be worse than any story he'd ever heard of the Great War.

In the next few hours, the three little fishing boats did what they could. The sailors were eternally grateful as they were hauled aboard, mainly to *Daisy II* which had been right in the thick of the action. By four o'clock John Gatt agreed with Robert and the Orcadian skipper that they could see no more survivors and it was time to give up. The *Royal Oak* had sunk almost immediately following the U-Boat strike, the oil from her fuel tanks spreading across the water of the Flow in a deadly black sheen. Some men had choked to death before anyone could reach them...

The boats sailed back to Kirkwall harbour by five o'clock. It was pitch dark now, the aurora having vanished. John Slater had almost forgotten about his injury, but once berthed, Robert ordered Sandy to take him to a doctor. By then another battleship had made it back, having heard the radio traffic from the *Daisy II* and the *Pegasus*. They had a surgeon onboard who was called away to look over the rescued sailors, but those who were uninjured were directed to the Fishermen's Mission, the doors of which had been opened by their Superintendent, on hearing of the tragedy. A local doctor came down from his house with the Superintendent and a few other early risers to provide some tea and blankets. When the Orcadian GP saw the state of John's mangled finger he told him to come into the kitchen so he could take a proper look.

"That's no' a bonny sight," the doctor grinned.

"I canna feel it though, Doctor," John said, as he sat down on a wooden stool.

"A blessin', then. Noo, put yer hand on the table and we'll see what we can do wi' it," the doctor instructed blithely, putting a teacloth down first. From his leather bag, the medical man extracted a surgical needle, a reel of catgut and a bottle of whisky. He then examined the torn skin and the stump of bone. "Hmm, that bone is cracked and the skin left is nae enough tae cover it, so I'll have tae break it off and sew ye up roon aboot the knuckle. It'll maybe still move, I canna tell hoo much damage has been daen tae the nerves, but we canna waste time, as it's still bleeding oot. It'll be painful, so I'll gie ye a big dram tae ease it, as I've nae ether tae give ye," he explained.

John narrowed his brows, looked up at his cousin who shrugged, and then shook his head. "Nah, nah, Doctor, I canna tak alcohol, I'm a teetotaller," he said gravely.

"But it's medicine, man! Ye need it! I'm going tae break off yer finger-bone, it'll be excrutating!" the doctor protested.

"Never een! I will nae let spirits pass my lips. I'm a fisherman, Doctor, I've fought wi the elements, a bittie pain winna kill me, you dae fit ye have tae, but I'm nae touching that glass!" John was adamant.

The doctor looked at Sandy for some support, but John's fair-haired cousin just smiled, "He's richt, oor village has taen a Temperance stand since 1843 fan the womenfolk marched tae the Broch tae protest aboot licenced premises being allowed in Cairnbulg. Oor grandfathers baith played in the Flute Band, as did oor faithers, and John here has been the drummer the last twa year, so ye winna convince him itherwise," Sandy explained politely.

"Well," the doctor sighed, ruffling his hair, "I've never heard the like!"

"Gie me anither cloth and we'll get goin'," John told him. The doctor took one from the sink and gave it to John with a curious look. Sandy held John's arm down on the table, and John stuffed the cloth in his mouth and bit on it. The doctor snapped the cracked bone in one swift movement; John stiffened and gulped rapidly, but the pain subsided as soon as it had flared. It was then a matter of the skin being trimmed and sewed together, which John found more ticklish than sore. Sandy had spend most of the time looking away, unable to focus on the messy process, but when he looked back, the doctor was cleaning up

John's hand with cotton wool, using a brown substance from a green ribbed bottle labelled *Lugol's Solution – 2% Iodine in Distilled Water*.

"Well, they say the North-East fishers are hardy men, but now I've seen it for masel'. Now you should keep that clean and see your own physician at hame, he'll need to remove the stitches in a fortnight," the doctor said.

"Aye, I'll do that, thank you, Doctor, ye made a bonny job," John told him, admiring the now tidy half of his pinkie which remained.

"And if you dinna need the water of life, I do!" the doctor laughed and poured a measure into the empty glass on the table, then took a long sip. John and Sandy thanked the doctor again and went back into the hall where the navy men were having tea.

"Ah, I heard we had another casualty, how did Dr Linklater do?" the man who spoke was the naval surgeon who had been aboard the *HMS Manchester*, one of the battleships which had been moved out of Scapa Flow as part of orders to disperse the fleet.

"A bonny job, sir, tak a look for yersel'," John told him, now feeling very weary from lack of sleep.

The surgeon examined the stitching, "Mm, yes, a very good job for a general practitioner!" he praised. Dr Linklater was just coming out of the kitchen and heard the surgeon's comment.

"Thank you, Dr Forbes, I widna want your job or conditions though, it's been a bad night. How many lost?" the Orcadian asked.

"At least seven hundred, very likely more, the officers who survived are making roll-calls, there were one hundred boy seamen, not even eighteen, this was the very first voyage for most of them," Dr Forbes replied gravely. "But we must thank you fishermen, we would have lost the entire crew without your help," he turned back to John and Sandy.

"John Gatt wis the real hero, sir, the skipper o' the *Daisy II*. He is fae the same village as us," Sandy spoke up.

"Indeed, I've just treated the *Royal Oak's* captain, he tells me he will personally be recommending that Mr Gatt's bravery be formally recognised. There were three hundred and eighty-six men brought onboard the Daisy II, and every one eternally grateful to Mr Gatt and his crew," Dr Forbes said.

"Aye? And well deserved that will be, Doctor, the Orcadians will never forget Skipper Gatt either!" Dr Linklater commented.

John looked at Sandy, "Well, if John Gatt gets a medal, I'll certainly hae my ain souvenir o' this nicht!" he said, and yawned, "We nott oor beds, Sandy, come on, oor skipper needs tae ken far we are," he added.

"Jist fit I wis thinking, let's get back tae wir boat," Sandy said.

"So that's what really happened? And I didn't know about the battleship, we haven't done much about World War II, only about the Blitz," James exclaimed.

"We'll get it in the academy, James, but wow, and Didey refused the whisky?" I said, knowing very well our grandfather's strong temperance views.

"Aye, he would never have touched it, nae even as an anaesthetic! They were brave men in a bygone day, I dinna think a young man o' nineteen would cope haen his pinkie broken and then sewed up with nae painkillers in the present time!" Uncle Sandy laughed. "See, you're nae gaun tae feel onything, they'll pit ye tae sleep, and ye'll be fine," he assured me. "And here's the doctor noo," he added as the surgeon and the nurse appeared.

"Hello, Miss Fraser, we're going to take you for your operation in a few minutes," the nurse said, putting on a cheery smile. "We'll give you something to make you sleep, it won't hurt, I promise," she said.

"Nurse, I'm eleven years old, I know you're going to give me a needle, it's ok, as long as I can see properly again after!" I told her glumly.

James gave me a big hug, he knew I was a little scared. "We'll be here when ye get back, sis, be brave!" he said. I hugged him back. This was one time I was happy he was here.

I felt the needle when the nurse poked it into my vein moments later, then it was the strangest feeling, like I was falling backwards, not just onto the bed, but down, down, into darkness, seeing James and Uncle Sandy's faces zip away from me. In that darkness I heard waves splashing, not wildly, but like on a gentle sea. Faces that were fuzzy pulled into sharp focus as I kept on falling. I recognised my great grandmother, Annie Duthie, one of the heroic James Duthie's daughters. She was young, as in her schooldays, her hair in long braided plaits, bouncing behind her back as she skipped along a sandy road. There was her sister Maggie, who had lived in her parents' house long after they passed away, and had died at a great age, having never availed herself of any modern conveniences. I heard my mother's voice, "Great Aunt Maggie died one hundred years after her parents' marriage, she was ninety-two. She was the last link with the bygone days that my Granny loved to speak of. Maggie Duthie was a Victorian, and her values never changed."

I felt tears on my cheeks, wishing I had known her. I had a vague memory of a very old lady in a black dress being present at James and I's fourth birthday, which was only a few weeks after Mary had been born. Was that Maggie? My great grand aunt? I concentrated hard, I wanted to see her face as she was then, the distinguished pensioner who dressed as if Queen Victoria was still on the throne. She had outlived her whole family, even her youngest sister, little Jenny, the surviving twin.

There had been a James in every generation because of the sacrifice their father had made, and my brother was the fourth. Then I saw him, my great-great grandfather, James Duthie, known as James Lawrie Duthie, because his mother was a Lawrence. He was tall and rugged, though had a slim frame. His eyes were a sea-green, gentle and kind like the summer waves dappled in seaware, safe and trustworthy. He was rowing the yole, as he did that fateful night when he had sacrificed his life to give his crewmates a chance to make their peace with God. I heard him singing, *"Will your anchor hold in the storms of life/ When the strong tides lift and the cables strain?"* Then everything faded away and silence fell like a black curtain.

CHAPTER 12

Canna believe it, my little sister getting marriet afore me! I'll hae to get the green garter, ye ken!" Annie Duthie said in mock anger. She had just thrown her arms around twenty-two year old Jenny, who had revealed that her boyfriend, Stuart Wood, had the previous night visited their maternal grandfather, Andrew Buchan, and asked permission to marry her.

"Oh, Annie, I'm sae happy! I never thocht ye could feel like this!" Jenny exclaimed.

"Well, I'm sure I'll feel the same if Sandy Slater ever gets his finger oot and asks me tae be his wife, but no, I am glad for ye, I aye worried aboot ye, kenin' that you came intae the world the day efter Da wis lost, and ...James oor brither left this scene o' time as weel. You aye acted as if James wis here fan you were a bairn, it sometimes feart me," Annie explained.

"But Annie, he always will be, he is part o' me, he's my twin, his spirit has aye been here fan I needed him," Jenny protested. "I think he'll rest noo though. Stuart and me are gaun o'er tae New Toon tae tell him oor news."

Annie had never liked her sister talking this way; as far as she was concerned, her father and little brother were in Heaven. They would only be reunited at the end of days, when the Lord had destroyed the old world and made the new for redeemed man to live in. Jenny was very like her mother in that respect, aware of the supernatural, keeping alive the old rituals and superstitions. Annie had explained it as Jenny's way of coping with never having known her father. "Aye, well, that's affa nice o' him. And he's a fisherman, that's a' ye need. Charlie may hae marriet a country woman, but we can keep the tradition goin'," she said.

"Mam's happy for ma, and so is Didey Andra, we'll go in by Didey Charlie and Granny Maggie efter we come back fae New Toon," Jenny said, smiling. Just then, there was a knock on the door; it was Stuart. He was tall, fair and had blue-grey eyes. He was not from the village, not even from Scotland, but from Whitby in East Yorkshire, yet it was a fisher town to the core. His great grandfather, a salmon fisher, had been born in

Burnbanks, a fisher enclave in Kincardineshire, not far from Stonehaven. Stuart had a mild Yorkshire accent, but this was perfectly acceptable with the locals as the Yorkshire dialect contained many similar words to the Cairnbulg one.

"How do, girls?" he said, smiling nervously.

"Come in, come in ye gype! Ye've nae need t' be feart at me!" Annie motioned with a wave of her hand. "So, ye're coming intae the family, eh? I hope you're nae takin' Jenny awa' doon tae Whitby, it's o'er far awa'!"

"Now fa's being feel? The New Toon railway mak's it much easier tae get hame, I could be in Whitby and be hame in a few oors," Jenny laughed, "But we hivna decided yet, it depends. Ye see, Stuart's the youngest o' his family, so his mither has an affa notion o' him, I dinna ken that she is keen tae let him awa' up here!"

"Well, we'll hae a problem then, cos Ma winna like you gaun awa' either, being oor youngest," Annie reminded her.

"We've been savin' though, I didn't want to ask ye till I knew we could afford t' have us own house," Stuart said, grasping Jenny's hand.

"See? He's a wise chiel!" Jenny said brightly. "We'll try tae get marriet at the end o' the spring, afore the herring go sooth. Cousin Arthur says that the Broch is getting a new harbour basin this summer, so there'll be affa disruption here then," she added. "Div ye think Mary would come doon for the weddin'?"

"I'm sure she would, Isabel-Iona will if her mither disna. She has a wee quinie of three, Patricia, ye could ask her tae be a flower-girl," Annie said.

Jenny turned to Stuart, "Oor cousin Mary bides in Shetland, her man owns a trawl fleet up there, their quine is the same age as me, her man is een o' the Frasers, aye, a cadet branch o' Lord Saltoun's family."

"Ah, I mind on you tellin' me, the cousin that gave birth among t' Travelling folk. Well, if we can manage t' feed them, ye can invite them!" Stuart said kindly.

"I'm sure it'll be the bonniest weddin' in Belger for mony a lang year. Mam will be back fae her fish-selling in nae lang so if you're gaun tae St Combs, ye better mak a move," Annie reminded them, casting a glance at the wooden mantle clock, whose hands were creeping towards four o'clock.

Stuart and Jenny walked hand in hand alongside the railway line towards St Combs. It was a bright afternoon, the first signs of spring were in evidence as little clumps of wild snowdrops poked their green stalks and white heads out of the damp grass. They entered the old kirkyard by the iron gate; Jenny had a sudden flash of memory, being carried in her mother's arms, following the little white coffin which was being carried by her male relatives. Jenny gripped Stuart's hand tighter.

"Are tha sure thou's happy coming here? I cannot help feeling sad for ye, Jenny. I cannot imagine what it would be like to lose any o' my brothers and sisters," he said softly.

"Dinna be sad my sweetheart, James is aye with me in spirit. We must tell him o' oor plans, especially if we are gaun tae move awa', jist tae pit him at rest," Jenny was smiling, but her heart ached. Stuart was the only person she had ever told of her frustration and anger at never being able to grow up with her twin or know her father.

"Well, tha knows I will do whatever thou asks," he replied.

They stood before the grave, right next to that of Jenny's grandmother, Jane Bruce Buchan, whom she had been named after. Little James' headstone was a plain marble slab with a curved top, but at the side of it stood a carved child-angel also in marble. It had been a gift from the local mason, who felt so keenly for their loss, his wife having had a stillborn child in the same year, that he had made this sculpture, replicating the one at his own baby's grave.

Stuart crouched down and patted the angel's head as he read the words *James Andrew Buchan Duthie, stillborn 31 March 1887, beloved son of James and Elizabeth Duthie of Cairnbulg, twin brother of Jane Bruce Buchan Duthie; brother of Annie, Charles and Margaret Duthie. Suffer the Little Children to Come Unto Me.*

"How do, little lad? A've come to tell thee that I want t' marry thy sister," he said softly, feeling the words choke on the lump of supressed emotion in his throat.

Jenny stood, she could feel very gradually the presence of her brother's spirit appearing beside them. She could always see him as a little boy, never the same age as her. Sometimes in her dreams she could see the baby, from those first few hours of her life, and was always convinced that he had lived for a few minutes at least. The spirit was faint, ethereal, but yes, he had come.

"Jamesy, this is Stuart, he's gaun tae be your new brither-in-law. We micht be gaun awa' doon tae his hame in Whitby tae bide, but we'll aye come back, just as brither Charlie has promised ye he will come an' a'," Jenny said. She saw the little spirit child come and wrap his little arms around Stuart as he crouched by the headstone.

"He's giving ye a bosie, he's happy for us," she exclaimed. Stuart could not see anything, but he felt inexplicable warmth and a feeling of peace. "Thank thee, little Jamesy, tha'll never be left alone, I promise it!" Stuart said aloud. Jenny could see that the ghostly child looked up and smiled. Stuart suddenly felt tears on his face, the sensation of another being there was immediately very strong. She was right, the little lad was there with her all the time.

Stuart jumped to his feet and embraced Jenny. She could feel his shoulders shaking with sobs. "Oh my darlin', now dinna greet, James is happy for us, he'll rest noo, dinna be sad," she assured, stroking his hair.

He looked at her, "I cannot take thee away from here, no, not as far as Yorkshire, it wouldn't be right!"

"Aye ye can, if yer mither canna bear you tae be awa', we'll bide in Whitby a few years, then come back fan oor bairns have grown, so nae mair worries, the deid are aye with us fan we need them, but I think James will be at peace noo, he disna need tae watch for me ony mair. Aww, ye're sic a saft loon! I love you, ye daft gype!" Jenny kissed his mouth triumphantly.

He pulled back, a little surprised at her open display of affection, but then held her close again. "Aye, daft as a brush, that's what ma father says about me!" He turned back to the stone angel, "Tha' sister will be safe wi' this boy from Yorkshire, ah can promise it, little lad!"

"Hey, did ye ken we hae English relations?" James asked.

We were at Uncle Sandy's on the Sunday after my eye-operation. James had been getting the benefit of all the usual family storytelling from Sandy and Didey John while I had been in hospital.

"Really? Oh jings, that's terrible!" I said. I am embarrassed that I was ever suspicious of people from south of the border, but in those days our primary school teachers taught a very black and white version of history. We had done the Scottish Wars of Independence last year and had a school trip to Bannockburn, and as far as we were concerned it was England vs Scotland.

"Don't be daft, these folk were from Yorkshire, it's ok, come on, you know how Didey has spoken about going to Scarborough and Whitby with the herring fishing, well, they are all towns in Yorkshire, so if they were fishers, they couldn't have been all that bad, eh? It was a great story! Jenny, our great-great grand aunt, the twin whose brother died when they were born, married a guy from Whitby called Stuart Wood. But his great-grandfather was from near Cove Bay! It all goes around in circles!" James enthused and proceeded to repeat the story of Jenny and her Yorkshireman, with which Didey had furnished him the second evening I had been in hospital.

"And did they go away to Whitby after the wedding?" I asked, having seen many postcards from there in the box of old photos.

"Well, nae right away. Look, I've got something to show ye. Uncle Sandy has copies o loads of the family certificates. Being the oldest, he's got the job of looking after the family Bible! It's huge, it's got brass clasps and it's bound in leather, and the family tree of the Duthies is written in the front of it. Didey John got it handed down to him when his sister and two brothers died. But anyway, look!" he urged, handing me an old, fragile piece of paper which was inside a plastic pocket.

"*Certificate of Death – Rathen Parish – Village of Cairnbulg*, oh James, don't tell me..." I began, fearing that there was another tragic story forthcoming, "*20th January 1910...*"

"Now Doctor, it's only my dother that's made me come tae see ye, I dinna want tae mak a fuss!" Betsy Duthie protested as she sat down on a chair opposite Dr Slessor in his consulting room in Fraserburgh.

"But you say you've been having headaches, Mrs Duthie, very severe ones, yes?" the doctor asked, gently. He was a very dapper man who wore a wing collar and ribbon tie under a fine tweed jacket and black moleskin trousers.

"Aye, it's nae fine, richt behind ma een. Is that nae fit they call migraines?" Betsy suggested.

"Possibly, but let me do a basic examination, Mrs Duthie, and I shall ask you some more questions. Dr Slessor checked Betsy's blood pressure, her heart and lungs, then felt around her forehead. He hummed and hahed, much to Betsy's great annoyance, surely she could get these new-fangled asprin tablets to help a sore head?

"Mrs Duthie, there's a lump just above your hairline, I'm a bit concerned about it, but in order to find out more, I believe it would be wise for me to refer you to the Royal Infirmary in Aberdeen to have an x-ray scan of your skull. This is a picture of the bones and muscle inside your head, it is much safer than when it was first developed almost fifteen years ago. It will allow the specialist to rule out any abnormalities," Dr Slessor said with a rather grim tone.

"An x-ray? Oh doctor, surely that's nae needed? Fit difference does a lump mak?" Betsy protested.

"We have to be on the safe side, Mrs Duthie, I think I would be happier from a professional point of view to refer you. If there is nothing wrong, then there will be no further need for concern and I can prescribe you some asprin," he told her, smiling.

"Fit is that gaun to cost?" Betsy had avoided doctors all her life; her children had all been born with the help of the howdie-wife. People in the village knew old remedies for every ill, but in this new century the younger generation seemed obsessed with the druggist and the doctor. "Let me worry about that, Mrs Duthie, if they find nothing, you would not owe me anything. Please, I feel I need to be insistent about this, especially as you said there was no lump there previously," Dr Slessor assured.

Betsy sighed, "Well doctor, I ken my bairns will all be willing tae help me if there are things tae be paid for, but dinna offer me false charity, I hae never owed ony man in my life." Just then there was a knock at the door. The doctor called "Enter," and in came Maggie Duthie.

"Oh, beg yer pardon, Dr Slessor, I only jist heard my mither was here," she said, breathlessly. "How are ye, Mam?"

"The doctor is saying I hae to go to Aberdeen Infirmary for an x-ray! Fit a fuss for nothing!" Betsy exclaimed.

"Mam, the doctor dis ken better!" Maggie retorted. "What is actually wrang with her, Doctor?" she turned to Dr Slessor.

"Miss Duthie, your mother has described symptoms of bad headaches and pain behind her eyes, ordinarily that indicates a migraine, but there is a lump that I am concerned about."

Maggie looked at her mother; yes, she had complained of sore heads and sore eyes, and occasionally complained of feeling sick, but the family had put it down to the excitement of Jenny's wedding, and perhaps even the thought of her youngest daughter's impending move to Yorkshire. Betsy was now fifty-two; her father had been ninety when he passed away, the Buchans all lived long, why should anything be wrong now? Maggie sighed, Betsy's eyes looked a little weary, and her skin was noticeably paler than usual. "Well, Doctor, if you think she needs attention at the Infirmary, we'll dae that," Maggie said eventually, a creeping fear beginning to manifest itself in the back of her mind.

Due to Dr Slessor having a telephone in his office, he was able to arrange an appointment in a matter of minutes. Betsy marvelled at his ability to communicate with unseen people in far off Aberdeen. "Aye, it's so different even in my lifetime, Doctor, the train wis a fairlie fan it came along, now ye can use a machine tae speak to some ither body fa ye canna see, yet ye can hear! This x-ray, it sounds droll, ye say it's like a photograph o' my skull?"

"Precisely so, Mrs Duthie. Only instead of developing fluid and ink, it uses electromagnetic waves. I used to find the concept alien myself, but now I've seen it, it is a boon to medical staff all over the known world! You have nothing to fear, my colleagues at Woolmanhill have some of the most advanced equipment in Scotland, and if anyone can diagnose the cause of your headaches correctly, they can."

Dr Slessor's endorsement gave Maggie some assurance. A week later, Maggie, Annie and Betsy travelled into Aberdeen on the train from Cairnbulg. Charlie met them at the station, having taken a few hours off work to accompany his family. They were able to take an electric tram from Union Street to Rosemount Viaduct and walk down behind the Public Library to the hospital. The area was crowded with houses, all stone tenements built out of the local granite. The Royal Infirmary itself was an impressive structure with a neo-classical design of recessed central pediments with large square blocks either side. "I aye thought it looked mair like an academy than a hospital, but that wis the genius o' Archibald Simpson, the man fa designed it," Charlie explained. "He created maist of the buildings in the city early last century."

"Well it's fairly imposing, Charlie!" his mother observed.

Soon they found the entrance and were met with long, tall corridors in a cream and green colour scheme. Charlie headed directly for the reception desk and stated that his mother had an x-ray appointment. The man at the desk gave him directions and they walked along one corridor and up a stair which had a large painted sign declaring Radiology Department. "This is where the mannie said to go," Charlie said, holding open the large wooden swing door. Eventually, after finding another glass-fronted reception room and consulting with the staff there, they found the waiting room for Betsy's appointment. Her name was called almost immediately, and she followed a nurse in a blue gown with white puffed sleeves which only came to the elbow and a pristine white apron and cap. "This is Dr Noble, he's going to take your x-ray, Mrs Duthie, nothing to worry about, it's all very simple," she said in a refined city accent.

"Ee well, Doddie Noble! I heard you'd gone in for a doctor, and here ye are, am I glad tae see ye!" Betsy exclaimed as she recognised one of her own classmates from St. Combs school. "It must be forty years since I've seen ye," she added.

"Betsy Buchan! It's a sma' world. I heard aboot James, I'm affa sorry, and your wee bairn, but that wis fan I newly came oot o' medical school. So, Dr Slessor wants us tae hae a lookie at that lump on your foreheid, and that's fit we'll dae," Dr George Noble said, taking her arm.

He took her through to a large room which had a huge piece of apparatus consisting of steel poles suspending something vaguely akin to a camera which had a huge bell-shaped lens holder. Under the bed which was positioned next to this structure was a huge grey steel box with coils of wire running between it and the camera. "Doddie, if you werena here, I wid be turnin' tail and running, fit is that monster?" Betsy whispered.

"It winna harm ye. This bittie here is the camera, picture starts tae appear on the plate fan the electricity passes fae the box under the bed. Ye micht hear the noise o' the generator, and the noise o' the lens cover openin', but that's a' there is tae it. Ye just nott a lie doon on the bed for aboot twenty minutes and I'll look at the photo, and send it back tae Dr Slessor. So, if you tak aff your coat, Nurse Wilson here will lay it on a chair for ye," George explained.

Betsy, trusting her old friend, removed her coat and hat, passing them to the well-spoken nurse, who seemed a little surprised at the doctor's familiarity. "He doesn't normally talk in Scots, that's the first time I've heard Dr Noble speak like that," she tittered.

"Well quine, there is naething like a hame voice tae pit yer fears tae rest, this man was in my class at school, the cleverest o' them a'. He came fae a little fisher cottage and his father and grandfather were baith fishermen, so fae humble beginnings he has proved ye can dae onything if ye set yer mind tae it, like my son, he is headmaster at the Grammar School up the road here!" Betsy told her proudly. The nurse seemed amazed, and made no further comment.

As she lay on the bed, looking up into the lens of the x-ray camera, her mind wandered. Seeing Doddie Noble reminded her of things she had forgotten. Time is indeed like a thief, far has it gone in my lifetime? I have been a daughter, a mother, and now a grandmother, is my span tae be less than the threescore and ten the Scriptures promise? Oh Lord, if that's true, gie me the strength tae cope, as ye aye have done. I fain would see my man again, and my little lost bairn, the family are a' able tae look efter themselves. But look efter Maggie, she disna seem tae want to find a man, she wis happy looking efter a' the auld folk, but now ma father's wi' ye as well, Lord, oh, mak her path plain to her...

"A lump?" Charlie whispered loudly, as Maggie repeated what Dr Slessor had told her.

"Aye, and you ken fit that means! I'm nae gaun tae say it, but it disna sound good," Maggie retorted.

Charlie sighed, "Maggie, they can operate on these things now, I've heard amazing stories o' how folk can be brocht back fae the deid mair or less. If it is... well, they will try their best, I'm sure!"

Annie had gone to look out of the window, unwilling to hear her siblings' speculations. Whirling around in her mind was her own relationship with Sandy Slater. Yes, they had been courting for many a year now, but why would he not ask her? She had hoped that being at Jenny's wedding would have prompted him. She resented the fact that Sandy's aged mother was a bullying harridan, and would not countenance her only child leaving her to marry. Now why could it happen this wye, that my mither might hae a tumor and yet that miserable auld carle is in her eighties and winna dee?

" 'Cause of death – brain tumor', oh James, she was only in her early fifties! How horrible for them all! But in 1909 they didn't know much about treating cancer, did they?" I sighed. What an awful tragedy! "You don't think anything will happen to Mum, do you? I mean, she's a bit old to be having another baby…"

"But then, medicine has advanced since Betsy died! Let's be logical," James had completed my thoughts as ever.

"Don't you ever get cancer! Or anything!" I told him firmly.

"Ha! I'm nae going anywhere. You'll get sick of me fan you're older and you've got a boyfriend!" he laughed.

"Oh no I won't, you'll be coming to me, begging me to ask girls out for you!" I said, and playfully hit him with a cushion. "James," I suddenly said, being serious, "I want to see the graves at St Combs cemetery, that's where they all are, Betsy, James, little James, and Betsy's parents. Let's ask Uncle Sandy to take us through to Didey's tonight. It's summer, it'll be light till at least ten, or even tomorrow, if he won't take us on a Sunday. We have to see them, they're part of us, part of our story!" I shall never know why that urge seized me just then, but I had the strongest desire to connect with my mother's family, because deep down, I suppose I was afraid of the same thing happening to the baby as had to Jenny Duthie's brother.

On that bright summer evening, Didey and Granny took us to the old kirkyard in St. Combs. It still stands to this day, looking out over the sea, where so many were lost, their grave the deep waters, but the headstones were there to remember them. We almost did not need direction, James and I were able to home in on the graves of our ancestors immediately. There was the little marble angel, much weathered, but showing evidence of being cleaned.

"Oh James, they were your namesakes!" I suddenly realised, reading the stone. *In memoriam - James Charles Duthie, father of the above, lost at sea 31 March 1887, aged 32 years. Here also lie Elizabeth Jane Buchan Duthie, mother of the above, died 5 January 1910, aged 53 years; Charles Duthie, brother of the above, died 1 March 1950, aged 74 years.*

James crouched down and looked closely at the words, stroking them with his fingers. "We had the lettering daen again a few years ago," Didey said as he and Granny stood back.

"Dide, is this why ye never said that it wis your grandfather that Andrew Cardno saw at the shore? Because he had my name? Because he died, hoping that Billy and George would be given another chance?" James asked, looking up.

I looked too. This was one of the few times I saw tears in my grandfather's eyes. He had become upset the first time he had told me the full story of the wraith, and now I felt his sorrow again.

"I never kent him, nor my granny, she wis awa' ten years afore I wis born. Yet I had ma Slater grandparents right up till I wis thirty year auld. Fan Uncle Charlie telt me the stories that my mither never wid, I bade him tak' me here, jist like ye've asked tae come the day. My bonnie bairns, I wis never sae pleased that ye bore the names o' my ain folk, and that ye're sae keen on hearin' the family stories. Noo I ken they will never be forgotten," Didey's voice cracked. Granny took hold of his hand without saying a word.

"May the Lord bless our sister Betsy and give us comfort for her loss," the words of Rev. Gillanders, the second minister since

Rev. Dr. MacGibbon, rang out in St Combs Kirkyard. He was from Inverness, but a fine man nonetheless, and he had been in the village long enough to know Betsy and her story. Charlie felt empty, even though his wife Rosemary held tight his hand, and their two children, James and Mary clung to their father. He knew it was inevitable after Dr Noble had shown him the x-ray and the large white mass in his mother's brain; an inoperable tumour which would give her maybe six weeks to live. Betsy had eschewed morphine, saying she didn't want to be 'away with the fairies' at the end. The little cottage, where Charlie remembered that last night with his father, had been filled with family at Betsy's last hour. She said she had seen an image of James, that it would soon be time.

Maggie pulled at her black velvet gloves as they stood in the kirkyard. She bit her lip to stop the tears coming. I'm the last in the hoose, now Annie is tae be wed, I maun bide there till the end! Maggie had never felt the need of marriage or children of her own, she had so many nephews, nieces and cousins she could take care of. But that house, there was a strong pull in it, and she could not leave it now. She recalled her mother's last words to her, "Maggie, I'm gaun tae be with yer father, and yer brither, we'll see ye again one day, never let the circle be broken!"

Jenny and Stuart stood by Jenny's family; they had postponed their move to Whitby after Betsy's illness had been made known. Jenny felt that everything had been wound up, there was no need for her to stay especially after the vision of her twin she had seen here not so long ago. Yes, she would be the first to admit she was superstitious, but now there was a peace that indicated there was no more need for the rituals and fears of the past.

Annie was not sure what to feel. Her mother's illness had prompted Sandy to defy his mother once and for all, which had resulted in the old woman breaking down in tears and admitting she feared being left alone. So they had assured her they had no intention of moving any further than Fraserburgh, where Sandy's trawler was berthed, and the wedding date had been set for the following spring.

Standing here now, hand in hand with her fiancé, Annie had a vivid memory of her brother's funeral. She and Charlie had been helped by their cousins to lower the little white coffin into the grave. It was strange how similar this day had been; Charlie

had taken charge, directing his male relations in carrying the

coffin across from the house to Inverallochy Kirk. She would

never ever forget his words when the hearse had reached St.

Combs. The ebony carriage which was drawn by two sleek black

horses drew to a halt at the head of the brae down to the

kirkyard. Patrick and Mary had organised the hire of this grand

vehicle, but Annie had been unaware that Charlie and his

brother-in-law had made a special arrangement with the

undertaker.

"Now boys," Charlie's voice was strong and clear,

carrying in the frosty air. The pall-bearers were Charlie himself,

Patrick, Betsy's brothers, Charles and John Buchan, and her

brother-in-law, George Bremner, James Duthie Snr's old

crewmate. "We will dae this last service for my mither and carry

her tae the kirkyard in the village o' her birth." Although

underfoot had been icy, the men had taken up the coffin on their

shoulders and made the solemn procession down through the

village, followed by the family, and many of those in St. Combs who knew Betsy, including Doddie Noble, who had been there at her passing a few days previously.

Now they all watched the black varnished coffin slip slowly into the grave as the men lowered it. Maggie felt the tears spring to her eyes then. Oh Mither, how can I carry on without you and Da? Then she felt a little hand slip into hers. She looked down expecting to see one of her cousin's children, but instead of a human child, Maggie realised she could see a faint image of a little boy with eyes exactly like her father's. *Jamesy? Is that you?* She thought.

Be strong, sister, we're a' safe at the eternal harbour. The voice she could hear in her head, but she knew no-one else could see or hear, it was a divine revelation just for her. She held up her face to the sharp winter sun and smiled. Thank you, Lord, that wis mair than I needed, but now I ken You can send your angels at ony time, even in the image o' the brither I never knew, was her silent prayer.

Rev. Gillanders pronounced the benediction and the crowd slowly dispersed. Maggie shook his hand, "Reverend, div

ye believe the Lord can send visions tae comfort us in time o'
need?" she said.

"Well, He did so in the time of the Scriptures, there is no
reason why He cannot now. I pray you will find the comfort you
need, Margaret," he replied.

Maggie walked back alone over the dunes by the railway.
She felt a lightness of spirit she had not known in her whole life.
She began to sing her father's favourite hymn, Will your anchor
hold in the storms of life... yes she would keep the stories of her
family alive, not one would forget how the fishers of Belger,
Cotton and New Toon lived, worked, worshipped and died in
this little north east corner.

EPILOGUE

Duncan Thomas Duthie Fraser was born on Bonfire Night, 1981. We could hear the squibs exploding and saw the coloured reflections of the fireworks in the sky on the hospital windows. Peterhead Cottage Hospital looks directly out onto the Links, a big grassy area next to the oldest part of the town, the Kirkburn.

Mum was relieved. She kept saying over and over "I thought I'd lose him, I thought he wouldn't make it." The nurse reassured her that it had been a textbook delivery, and there was no more to worry about. When we came through to the ward, baby Duncan was all clean and pink, with a knitted blue hat covering his wisps of baby hair. Uncle Sandy had taken us down to the hospital from their house.

"See, fit did I tell ye, Betsy? You worry far too much, jist like your granny Annie Duthie Slater!" Sandy teased his sister lightly.

"Worrying is a fisherwoman's trait, *Alexander*, and I'm sure your wife knows that!" Mum had retorted, but she was smiling.

"Mum, he's so cute!" Mary cooed, as baby Duncan grabbed tightly at her finger.

"Aye, yes, and you've to be a grown-up, May, you're not the baby now!" Mum told her. Dad patted Mary's head as if to say she would always be his baby girl.

James and I marvelled, having forgotten what it was like when Mary was a baby. Duncan's little face was round and soft; when he opened his eyes they were a greenish-blue. Yes, there was a trace of the Duthies in there, I thought.

"Mum, where did you get the name Duncan from? It isn't in the family that I know," I said, having digested as much genealogical information as I could from Didey and Sandy's collection of certificates.

"Ah, well, it isn't, right enough, but it's a fine Gaelic name, it means *brown haired warrior*. I learned Gaelic from being a hillwalker when I was young. But he has both Duthie and Fraser in his name, so he'll know his heritage, I'm sure," Mum explained.

"Oh we'll keep our brother right," said James.

"Of course we will, we know all the stories now, don't we?" I added, finishing his line of thought.

"Of that I have no fear," began Dad, "You two are definitely the storytellers of the family. Jings, I should tell you the history of the Frasers, my folk are descended from a cadet branch of Lady Saltoun's family."

James and I looked at each other and beamed. It was the beginning of a whole new story.

THE END

The twins will return in Book 2 with more stories of Fish and Folk

Glossary

Unless otherwise stated, these are all Scots words, specific to NE Scotland fishing communities

ahint:	behind
Auld Hornie:	the Devil, Satan
bairn:	child/ baby
beets:	boots
Belger:	traditional name for the village of Cairnbulg
box-bed:	bed in a wooden recess; common in traditional fishing & crofting communities
carle:	old woman/ also a common surname in NE Scotland
codling:	immature cod fish
contermashious:	contrary, argumentative, grumpy
Cotton:	Traditional nickname for Inverallochy, because of the cotton/hemp fields which reputedly grew

	there (see the description of the 'Hemplins')
creel:	woven u-shaped basket to transport fish, carried by the older women by means of a calico strap across their shoulders and chest.
curly-tail:	taboo name for pig
Didey:	Grandfather
dilly:	Traveller word for girl, young woman
dowp:	bottom
fairlie:	something out of the ordinary
feartie:	scared person
feel:	fool/foolish, crazy
Flushing Park:	name of the farm just outside Cairnbulg village; still exists today, displayed on OS maps as 'Flushing'
gadgie:	Traveller word for a man
galloot:	idiot, careless/clumsy person
gart/ gar:	caused to, e.g. fit gart him dae that? what caused him to do that?

govey dicks:	an exclamation of surprise, disgust or annoyance, depending on context
greet/ greetin':	cry/ crying
gype:	silly person
Ha'af fishing:	open-sea fishing carried out by Shetland men as part of their duties to their landlord who owned their houses and boats. The latter were called 'sixareens'
haddies:	haddocks
hallirackit:	bedraggled/ out of control
havering/ havers:	talking nonsensically/ nonsense
Hogmanay:	New Year's Eve in Scotland
Howdie-wife:	traditional midwife with no formal medical training
lappy:	taboo name for rabbit
lintie:	linnet/ any songbird
loon:	boy
lowing:	of a flame, glowing, burning
lugs:	ears
maun:	must

mootie:	Shetland term of affection, usually 'peerie mootie', meaning cute little thing or child
muckle:	large/ a great quantity
nae mowse:	traditional expression meaning not wise, unbelievable or even dangerous
nesmore:	Traveller word for mother
nickum:	rascal, cheeky child
nott:	need/ require
nyaff:	rascal, troublemaker
peerie:	Shetland word for little
quine:	girl
rannie hantel:	Traveller name for noble or gentleman/ used collectively for the gentry or landowning class
scrieves:	writes
throwe-come:	ordeal
verra dab:	very thing
Wast Shall, Dusky	actual names of fishing grounds which are approximately six to eight miles NE of Fraserburgh's Kinnaird Lighthouse

Whalsa':	Whalsay, Shetland Islands
wrack:	seaweed
yokit:	get started as regards work; from farming terminology, e.g. he yokit the cuddy, i.e. he yoked the horse.
yole:	traditional small fishing boat

Other works by the author:

All the Sinners Saints – a Novella

A Different Gunpowder Plot – Poetry Collection

These titles are available on Kindle.

You can follow Janet on Twitter **@JanetSwan73**

or 'Like' her Facebook Page

https://www.facebook.com/janetoferryhill

3373299R10143

Printed in Great Britain
by Amazon.co.uk, Ltd.,
Marston Gate.